Finding Sophie

IRENE N. WATTS

Tundra Books

Published in Canada by Tundra Books,
481 University Avenue, Toronto, Ontario M5G 2E9

Published in the United States by Tundra Books of Northern New York,
P.O. Box 1030, Plattsburgh, New York 12901

Library of Congress Catalog Number: 2002101143

National Library of Canada Cataloguing in Publication Data

Watts, Irene N.
Finding Sophie

ISBN 0-88776-613-7

I. World War, 1939-1945 – Refugees – Juvenile fiction.   2. Jewish girls –
England – Juvenile fiction.   I. Title.

PS8595.A873F55 2002   jc813'.54   C2002-900798-4
PZ7.W336Fi 2002

We acknowledge the support of the Canada Council for the Arts and the
Ontario Arts Council for our publishing program.

We acknowledge the financial support of the Government of Canada
through the Book Publishing Industry Development Program for our
publishing activities.

Design: Blaine Herrmann

Printed and bound in Canada

This book is printed on acid-free paper that is
100% recycled, ancient forest friendly (40% post-consumer recycled).

1 2 3 4 5 6   07 06 05 04 03 02

For Sarah Elizabeth Duncan

ACKNOWLEDGMENTS

Thanks to my editors at Tundra: Kathy Lowinger, who asks the right questions, and Sue Tate, for her patience and careful copyediting.

Also to my daughter Julia Everett, who converts early ideas and writing into a readable manuscript, and to Catherine Mitchell, for her ongoing support.

Heidenröslein. Words by Johann Wolfgang von Goethe, 1771. (1749-1831).
Music by Franz Schubert, 1815. (1797-1828).

Prologue

THE TRAIN, BERLIN, GERMANY
DECEMBER 1, 1938

Just before the guard reached their compartment door, a woman threw in a rucksack, then lifted a little girl and stood her beside Marianne. "Please look after her! Thank you." She moved away without looking back.

One of the boys put the little girl's rucksack on the rack for her.

"Thank you," she said. "I'm Sophie Mandel. I'm seven."

After lunch they practiced English phrases and taught Sophie to say, "The sun is shining."

At the Dutch border, the Gestapo came on board. An officer pointed to the luggage. "Open up," he ordered.

The children put their suitcases on the seat for inspection. The Gestapo officer, with a quick movement, overturned each case and rifled his black-gloved hand through the contents. He pulled out Werner's stamp album and flicked carelessly through the pages, then put the album under his arm.

The officer stepped deliberately on Brigitte's clean white blouse, which had fallen to the floor. Josef's prayer shawl was thrown aside. Sophie's doll was grabbed, its head twisted off. Then the officer turned the doll upside down and shook it. Sophie cried quietly.

After the officer left, Brigitte twisted the doll's head back onto the neck and said, "Good as new," and handed the doll back to Sophie.

LIVERPOOL STREET STATION, LONDON, ENGLAND
DECEMBER 2, 1938

"Come on, Sophie, keep up," said Marianne as they walked along the platform to the waiting room to meet their sponsors. She could see some women talking about them and shaking their heads, the way mothers do when their child has been out in the rain without a coat.

"See them poor little refugees."

"What a shame."

"Look at that little one. Sweet, isn't she?"

"More German refugees, I suppose. Surely they could go somewhere else?"

"We'll have to try to speak English all the time," Marianne told Sophie, taking her hand.

"But I don't know how. I want to go home," Sophie said.

Marianne was too tired to answer.

*   *   *

The woman in charge called: "Sophie Mandel."

"That's you, Sophie. Come on, you've got to wake up."

"Hello, Sophie," said a lady in gray, picking up the rucksack at Sophie's feet. "I am Aunt Margaret, a friend of your mother's. I've come to take you home."

Sophie put her arms around Marianne's neck and hugged her, as if she didn't want to leave her behind.

"Good-bye Sophie. She looks very nice," Marianne whispered and kissed her cheek.

· I ·

Do people know the precise moment when their lives change? All I know is that, for me, it happened just before my fourteenth birthday.

I've had six birthdays in England, five of those in wartime, and now at last everyone says peace is just around the corner. It's hard for anyone my age to remember a time before blackouts and rationing and bombing. I think of peace as being like one long holiday.

Unless you count being evacuated, I've only ever had one real holiday. It was the last summer before the war. I think it must have been August 1939. I was eight. Aunt Em – that's what I call Aunt Margaret – and I went to Brighton and stayed in a brown-and-cream painted boardinghouse near the beach. She bought me a bucket and spade and a red bathing suit. I built elaborate sand castles all day long and Aunt Em rented a striped deck chair and sat with the mothers, who watched the children. I got sunburned and my back peeled, so did Aunt Em's nose.

There was a pier with a puppet show. We ate ice-cream cones and I had a ride on a merry-go-round on a shiny pony with black leather stirrups. Aunt Em taught me a nursery rhyme:

> I had a little pony,
> His name was Dapple Gray;
> I lent him to a lady
> To ride a mile away.

At night the pier lit up with thousands of colored lights. We walked along it before I went to bed, and I sang all the way back to the boardinghouse.

I remember the salt water splashing my face when I jumped up and down in the knee-high waves. I remember my first taste of fish-and-chips, sprinkled with brown vinegar, which we ate straight out of the newspaper wrapping and not off plates. The sun shone every day, just like the first English sentence I'd learned, which was, "The sun is shining."

When we got back to London, I drew everything in a sketchbook Aunt Em let me choose in Woolworth's. I've still got some of those drawings.

Funny how everything about that week is so clear. If I go further back, there are lots of gaps. I don't remember much about the journey to England, or about my mother and father who stayed behind in Germany. They seem like photographs you haven't seen for a long time. You can't quite recall where they were taken, or who all the people are – they're like figures in a dream. By the time you wake up, most of the dream's evaporated.

I haven't heard from my parents since before the war – six years. I'm not sure how I know, or who told me, but my father's Jewish and my mother isn't. He used to call her Lottie, which is short for Charlotte. I've almost stopped missing them.

I did wonder at first what happened to Marianne – the girl who took care of me on the train to England. For a while I pretended she was my sister, and that one day she'd come and live with Aunt Em and me. In the beginning I didn't know the words to tell Aunt Em about her, and so Marianne began to fade away.

On the first night, when I arrived in London, Aunt Em tucked my doll into my bed with me. I screamed and screamed.

"Why, Sophie? Tell me what's wrong."

I hurled Käthe across the room. I refused to have her near me. I never wanted to play with or own a doll again. Next day we went to a toy shop and Aunt Em bought me a furry gray monkey, which I loved passionately. He still sits on my desk.

The last time I consciously thought about Marianne was when Aunt Em waved me good-bye at Paddington Station, two days before war broke out, in September 1939. I half expected to see

Marianne lining up with all the other school children who were being evacuated to safe places too.

Once we had boarded the train, the guard walked up and down the corridor outside our compartment and I hid under the seat with Monkey, afraid the guard would steal him.

"Did you lose something, Sophie?" my teacher asked. "You don't want to arrive in the country looking all dusty, do you?"

Mandy and Nigel Gibson, red-haired twins my senior by three weeks, promptly joined me under the seat. "She's looking for her pencil, Miss," they said in unison. "We're helping her." We've been best friends ever since.

Evacuation was a miserable experience for all three of us. The twins were separated. Mandy told Nigel she wasn't getting enough to eat, so he stole food for her from his foster mother's larder, got found out, and was beaten.

I was put with an old couple who spoke to me only when necessary, and reminded me daily to be grateful that they were giving me a home. I talked to Monkey a lot.

We lasted six months before Mrs. Gibson and Aunt Em brought us home.

It was still the "phony" war. Air raids hadn't started. When the Blitz proper began, Aunt Em murmured about sending me to a safe place. Instead she ordered a Morrison shelter, which had an iron top, mesh sides, and served as both a dining room table and a comfortable and safe place in which to sleep if air raids continued all night.

Mrs. Gibson had her cupboard under the stairs reinforced, and the twins stayed home too.

The person who's cared for me since I was seven is Aunt Em. Her real name is Margaret Simmonds – Miss Margaret Simmonds. We're not actually related.

She explained it very carefully: "I'm your temporary guardian, Sophie, which means I protect you and take care of you because your parents live in Germany. One day you'll live with them again."

When I started school, the girls asked me, "Is that your gran?" I wanted Aunt Em and me to belong together, so I told them she's my aunt.

"Did you know we have the same initials, Aunt Em?" I asked her. "Only they're in a different order. My first name starts with the same letter as your last – S – and my last name starts the same as your first – M – Sophie Mandel." I sort of hoped she might suggest I change Mandel to Simmonds. Sophie Simmonds sounds a lot more English. I never liked having a German name. Once the war began, I never spoke German again, and now I've forgotten it all.

One night the sirens wailed for the third night in a row, so Aunt Em brought her photograph album for me to look at in the Morrison shelter. "It will keep our minds off the war," she said. But it couldn't shut out the noise of the planes and the ack-ack guns trying to shoot them down, or the thump of the bombs not so very far away, but it helped.

"I was the only girl in the family. Don't I look solemn? I was seven when this was taken," said Aunt Em.

"Well, you're not solemn now," I replied.

Aunt Em has a lovely smile, and her brown hair is only a little bit gray. She wears it twisted into a bun. You can see it's naturally wavy.

"Who are the boys standing beside you, Aunt Em?"

"The tall one is Gerald; you've met him. He's my eldest brother. He lives in a village in Suffolk, in the house where I was born. This little boy is William, my youngest brother. He was my favorite."

We put our hands over our ears as bombs exploded nearby.

"What happened to him?" I asked, when the noise had died away.

"He was a soldier in the First World War. He died on the Somme, in France, in 1915."

"I'm sorry. Poor Aunt Em. Is this a brother, too? He looks very handsome."

"That's Robert, the boy who lived next door. We were all great friends. Sometimes the boys got tired of me tagging along when they went fishing, but I could beat them all at tennis."

"You liked him a lot, didn't you, Aunt Em? What happened next?"

"Robert and I got engaged when I was eighteen. He was killed in France, two years after William. At Passchendaele."

"Please don't be sad, Aunt Em."

"I'm not. It happened a long time ago, Sophie."

A long single note sounded. "There's the all clear. Off to bed, now. School tomorrow, and I have lots of new recipes to test for Lord Woolton."

Aunt Em works for the Ministry of Food. The Ministry rations food, and distributes pamphlets to help people make it go further. Aunt Em tries out all the new recipes on me. Sometimes they're quite disgusting. I think carrot marmalade was the worst. Not even Nigel Gibson would touch that and he devours almost anything.

"Tell me about one more, please, Aunt Em," I said.

"One more." Aunt Em turned the page of the album.

"After Gerald married Winifred, I decided to move to London to train as a secretary. I bought this little house with a small inheritance from my parents, and settled down.

"In 1928, I traveled to France. I wanted to see the country where William and Robert were buried. Then I hired a bicycle and toured Germany. The countryside there was quite lovely.

"At a youth hostel I met your parents and we became good friends. This is a picture of your mother and me standing outside Heidelberg Castle. I'd forgotten how much you resemble her. Your hair is fair, just like hers, but your eyes are brown like your father's."

It was strange to think that laughing girl, her arms linked with Aunt Em's, was my mother.

"Your father took the photograph, Sophie. It was the evening before your parents announced their engagement. They were so happy. He was going to work for a famous firm of architects in Berlin. When Hitler came to power, he wasn't allowed to work

7

there anymore. Your mother wrote me later that he became a landscape gardener.

"After I returned to England, your mother and I corresponded – we became pen friends. She and Jacob invited me to their wedding, but of course I couldn't afford to go to Europe again so soon. Later, much later, after you came along, she loaned you to me to take care of."

Loaned, like a book from the library?

I went to sleep thinking, *you have to take books back to the library, but I never want to be taken back and leave Aunt Em.*

· 2 ·

M andy calls for me as usual on Friday – our film-going night. This time next week, I'll be fourteen.

"Don't forget to keep the wireless on, Aunt Em. The war may be over before we get home."

"I hope you won't be that late, girls. Have a good time."

There was a long queue outside the pictures – there always is. The film was *Cover Girl*, with Rita Hayworth and Gene Kelly.

Mandy and I had long ago settled on our favorite male dancers.

"No one is as elegant as Fred Astaire," I insist.

"Can you imagine Fred jitterbugging? Gene Kelly invents a whole new style. By the way, Soph, has Nigel said anything to you yet?"

"About what?"

"About the Youth Club Victory Dance."

"I know there's going to be one – a costume dance as soon as Victory's announced. I'm helping with the decorations."

Mandy's left eyebrow goes up in the mysterious manner she's been practicing. It makes her look a bit like Harpo Marx. I don't comment.

"Swear you won't tell, but the other night when Mum was working the late shift, Nigel asked me to teach him how to waltz, and sort of mumbled that he might ask you to go with him to the dance."

"In that case I will decline any other invitations that might come my way," I say grandly, and we both burst out laughing.

"Do you remember when we were about eight, we swore we'd live in the same house when we were grown up, and I decided you'd have to marry Nigel as I couldn't?"

"You were always a bossy boots, Amanda Gibson. By the way, what did you cook for supper tonight? It was your turn, wasn't it?" I changed the subject deliberately – learned how to do that from Aunt Em.

"I opened a tin of unknown species of fish and we had it on toast. Nigel gave his to next door's cat. What did you have?"

"Aunt Em's Woolton pie, our Friday night special – anything that's left over from the week's meals baked with potato on top. I'm famished. Do we have enough money to buy chips on the way home?"

We pool our resources.

"If we share. We'll have to hurry after the show; they sell out early on Friday nights. When the war's over," Mandy says dreamily, "I'm going to live on bananas. With custard, or ice cream, or mashed with sugar, or sliced on white bread and butter."

The GI standing in front of us in the queue turns round and winks. "Can't have our allies starving," he says, in that wonderful slow American drawl. "Here, have some chocolate." He offers us a bar each.

Riches! Mandy and I look at each other hesitatingly. We're getting a bit too old to accept sweets from strangers.

"Go ahead, my intentions are honorable, right, hon?" The blonde girl with him puts her arm through his possessively.

"Thank you very much, Sergeant."

He turns away with a smile.

The *Pathé Gazette* news comes on after the big picture and before the cartoons. It shows English and U.S. forces liberating concentration camps. Dead bodies in heaps. Living dead. Bones barely covered with bits of striped rags, or huddled under shreds of blankets. Eyes staring from skulls peering through tiers of bunks, or pressed against barbed wire fences. I don't want to look, but can't turn away. *Are they real, or are they waxwork figures like those in the torture chamber at Madame Tussaud's?*

We leave before the cartoons. Mandy won't look at me. We hold hands all the way home, the way we used to when we were little. Neither of us speak.

I let myself in and hang up my mackintosh.

"I'm in the kitchen, Sophie," Aunt Em calls out. "You're home early."

"I'm not feeling very well," I say, and slump down beside her at the kitchen table.

"Shall I get you an aspirin, dear?" Aunt Em measures the sleeve of the cardigan she's knitting.

"Don't fuss, Aunt Em, I'm all right." I sense her looking at me as if she hadn't noticed that I'd snapped at her.

"I'm going to make some cocoa before I go to bed. Would you like a cup?" she asks.

I burst into tears.

Aunt Em rolls up her knitting and puts it away neatly in the old prewar tapestry knitting bag. "Do you want to tell me what's wrong, Sophie?"

I blow my nose. "Mandy and I were larking about in the queue, complaining about our starvation diets, and an American sergeant gave us chocolate. Oh, Aunt Em, it was awful." I put my half-eaten bar on the table.

"The chocolate?"

I'm not in the mood for jokes. "All those people dead, or dying in ways I haven't even heard of. They showed camps. Concentration camps – Belsen and Buchenwald. I'll never forget their names, or what's there."

"Yes. I heard a war reporter on the BBC earlier."

Aunt Em measures the cocoa powder into two mugs, adds a dash of milk and a bit of sugar, stirs, and pours on boiling water.

How can Aunt Em stand there and make cocoa?

She continues quietly: "I remember a broadcast I heard many years ago. It was given by Lord Baldwin in 1938. He was trying to get help for children in danger from the Nazis. Children who were Jewish or half Jewish, or whose parents were politically opposed to Hitler. He wanted English people to give homes to those children."

"Like you did?"

"Yes. I wrote down what he said: 'It's not an earthquake, not a famine, not a flood, but an explosion of man's inhumanity to man.' I wanted to help. It wasn't enough, obviously. How could we let it happen?" She sighs and puts her arm around me for a moment. "War and its atrocities."

I have a feeling she was thinking about that other war – the First World War.

"If you don't mind, I'll take my cocoa upstairs with me, Aunt Em."

Does Aunt Em realize how mixed up I feel? How can she? I can't even explain it to myself.

Every time there's been an air raid, every time someone in school hears of a brother shot down over enemy territory, or a father wounded or missing, I feel sad – guilty, too. Sometimes in Assembly when the headmistress says, with a sorrowful note in her voice, that something's been stolen from the cloakroom, or broken, and she hopes the guilty person will do the honorable thing and own up, I always go red, even though it's nothing to do with me. The trouble is, this *is* to do with me – I was born on the enemy side. Owning up's not going to change that. If only the war would end, if only we could forget all about it. . . .

I wish I'd been born right here in this narrow old house with its tiny back garden, almost too small for our vegetable patch, where we grow carrots and brussels sprouts. Where the apple tree's wormy and the blackberries have to be picked from the bush the minute they are ripe, or birds and hungry little boys eat the lot.

My bedroom's next to Aunt Em's, and there is a tiny spare room next to it, for a visitor or a maid. There isn't a maid, though. There's old Mrs. James, who comes in now and again to give everything a "good turnout."

The visitor's room is full of boxes of pamphlets and Red Cross supplies: blankets and patched sheets and secondhand clothes that Aunt Em collects for people in hospital or for blitzed families. She's been a member of the Women's Voluntary Services since 1939.

I love my room. The ceiling slopes down towards the bed and the window's opposite, set back in an alcove and crisscrossed with tape, in case of splintering glass. Sometimes at night, before I go to sleep, I draw back the blackout curtains. Not for long, though, because I'm afraid I might fall asleep, and wake up in the night and switch on the light and give enemy planes a target to aim for.

The walls are painted yellow to make the room look sunny. We're lucky to have walls. Incendiaries fell at the other end of the street, homes collapsed, people we know were hurt, and there was a lot of fire damage.

Aunt Em gave me her old desk – the one she used when she was my age, at her home in Suffolk. There are a couple of little cubbyholes for anything really private. I don't keep a diary –

drawing's easier for me than writing. I'm down to my last decent pencil. It's almost impossible to get good drawing pencils. I use mine to the last stub. Wish I still had one of those shiny ones. Can't get them anymore; everything's utility.

There's a print of Van Gogh's bedroom on one wall. It inspires me. Every line means something – tells me about the artist and the character or object he painted. A simple wooden bed covered with a red quilt, two chairs, bare floors, and shuttered windows. *How does he get that quality of light?* Uncluttered and complete.

My other picture is a watercolor called the *Post Office, Clovelly.* It shows a village painted by English artist Arthur Quinton, who lived in London till he died in 1934. I wonder if Clovelly was his favorite holiday place? The streets are cobbled. Two little girls in long dresses covered by white pinafores and wearing sunbonnets are walking up the hill. Behind them is the sea. There are railings in front of the houses. In London railings were given away long ago for the war effort. There's a striped awning over the post office, which has postcards for sale outside. A man leads a donkey, weighed down by panniers, toward the sea. A fishing boat bobs in the distance. Most nights this picture makes me feel safe and calm.

Aunt Em teases me because I can go to sleep anytime. She says the first time she saw me in Liverpool Street Station, I was asleep.

Tonight I can't stop thinking. *What if I hadn't been one of the children brought to England before the war? Where would I be? Where are my parents? Does my father have to wear a yellow star like some of those people on the news?*

The last and most important "where" – the one I keep pushing aside and which won't go away – is, *where am I supposed to belong? Where am I going to live when the war's over? Here with Aunt Em in my real life? Or with my parents, who are practically strangers, whom I can hardly remember?*

· 3 ·

Every time I close my eyes, I imagine I hear my wardrobe doors opening. Inside are rows and rows of dead bodies stacked up – one on top of the other. Skeletons wearing striped jackets, with six-pointed stars sewn over their hearts.

I get out of bed, make sure the blackout's in place. Then I switch on the light. The Van Gogh looks as if it's shifted a bit on the wall. I take it down. The nail's come loose. I'd better not hammer it back tonight. I put the print on the table next to the cocoa – there's skin on top. I drink it anyway. Can't bear to waste something with sugar in it. Actually, cocoa's not bad cold.

I sit cross-legged on my bed and look at the clean square of yellow paint – much brighter than the rest of the wall – where the Van Gogh normally hangs.

A long time ago there was a cream-colored wall in another room. . . .

A little girl sits cross-legged on the floor and looks for hours at a picture of a horse standing on the edge of a yellow cornfield, surrounded by emerald green hedges. The horse is red and tosses its blue mane, flicks its blue tail. The girl's papa gave the picture to her mother when they got married. It hangs on the wall of their living room.

At school the teacher says, "Draw something beautiful, so that the Führer will be proud of you." Herr Schmidt always walks up and down between the rows of desks. His breath smells of tobacco. His fingers are stained yellow as though he's been painting. He stands at his table and the pointer makes a singing noise in the air before it hits the edge. When he does that, someone's in trouble.

"Zoffie Mandel, bring your picture to the front. Turn around and face the class; show them your drawing."

The girl curtsies and does as she's told. *Her picture is beautiful. No need to be afraid.*

"What is this a picture of, children?"

"A horse, Sir."

"A horse. What color is this horse, children?"

"Red and blue, Sir," the class responds.

Has she done something bad? The colors aren't smudged. She hasn't gone over the lines.

"Who has seen a red and blue horse before? No one. Good. What color are horses, Magda? Yes. Black. Peter? Brown. Very good. Mathias? White. Excellent."

Her arms are getting tired. She needs to go to the toilet.

"Tell us, Zoffie, what color is *your* horse?"

The children scent trouble. They're glad it's someone else and not them.

"Speak up, I can't hear you."

The girl whispers, "Red and blue, Sir."

The class explodes into laughter. The pointer sings before it hits the wood.

"Silence! Hand me your picture."

The girl watches him tear it in half and throw it into the wastepaper basket. It is not over yet.

"This picture is an insult to the Führer. This is a bad picture. Where did you see this horse?"

"In a frame, Sir, in a room."

"What room, may I enquire?"

Even then, at six, she knows she must not tell the truth.

"I can't remember, Sir, just a room."

"Hold out your hand. Liar!" The pointer sings loudly before it stings her fingers. "Stand in the corner for the rest of the morning. Tomorrow, move your things to the back. Next to Samuel Bermann."

More laughter. Fingers pointing. The girl stands facing the wall. *She can't hold out much longer.*

After the bell rings for the end of school, some children chase after the girl, chanting, "Zoffie Mandel wet the floor. Zoffie Mandel sits with Jews. She's a dirty Jewish . . ."

She doesn't know the last word they call her.

When the girl gets home, she curls up on her bed. Papa built the bunk for her in the living room. He said it was like a bed on a ship. Her own little room inside the big one. She draws the curtains and falls asleep in the half-darkness of her bunk.

After Mama comes home from work, she tells her what the teacher said. Mama takes the picture down from the wall. There is a big clean patch where the horse used to be. When Papa comes home, Mama shouts at him: "Give it away, burn it. Suppose it's on the banned list? I've told you over and over we have to be more careful. The child talks. What is to become of you? Of all of us? We are a target."

"What shall I buy you instead? A picture of the Führer?"

"Are you deaf and blind?" Mama's voice quivers.

The girl covers her ears; she does not want to hear her mother crying. She wishes she could hide in the yellow cornfield.

After supper, Papa goes out. He takes the horse away, wrapped in newspaper, and the photograph of his family, whom she has never met.

Next day, when Mama comes home, she carries a big mirror in a gold frame. Four fat little gold angels decorate each corner. Papa hangs the mirror on the wall. He's tired from cutting the hedges outside the big houses along the Grunewald pine forest. He lies down.

"Doesn't the mirror look beautiful, Zoffielein?"

"Yes, Mama." The little girl misses the red horse.

"Listen carefully. This mirror was a christening present from your Grandmother Weiss."

"Grandmother? I have a grandmother?" the girl asks her mother. "Why doesn't she come to see me?"

Mama says, "You've forgotten. I told you about her. She lives far away in Dresden – she can't come to visit."

The girl wants to ask, may she send her a letter? Perhaps her grandmother will write back. Papa appears in the doorway, puts his finger on his lips. The girl does not ask any more questions.

Later, before she goes to sleep, Mama reminds her, "How long have we had this mirror, Zoffie?"

"A long time."

"Good girl," Mama says. "Do you remember who gave it to us?"

"The grandmother who lives far away."

I reach for my sketchbook. Only two clean pages left. Aunt Em gives me a new one every birthday. As soon as paper began to get scarce, she must have bought a supply of sketchbooks for me.

I draw the horse, color in the red body and blue mane and tail. Then I rough in the hedges. My green isn't quite the right shade, but close enough. The yellow cornfield gleams like the sun. I sign my initials. S.M.

Zoffie doesn't exist anymore. I'm Sophie Mandel. I draw the way I want to.

I switch off the light and go to sleep.

· 4 ·

Friday, April 27, 1945. My fourteenth birthday. Mandy's right, I do feel more grown-up. Lots of girls our age have left school and gone out to work.

Aunt Em went to the office extra early, so she could finish the new pamphlet on cooking potatoes in twenty-five different ways. They're one of the few foods that aren't rationed.

She made me the most beautiful birthday card. She used tiny scraps of leftover fabric from the quilts she makes for forces' convalescent homes.

I'm supposed to go to the butcher's on my way home from school. Good thing Aunt Em left the ration books out. I would *not* be happy queuing and then not getting anything because I'd forgotten them.

I hate going to Billy's Best Meats. His real name is William Billy. He always makes me think of the *Three Billy Goats Gruff* –

not the goats, but the troll. *Who's that going into my shop?* His teeth are very pointed, as if he's been gnawing on bones, sharpening his incisors.

I may declare myself a vegetarian, then I'd get extra cheese, and wouldn't have to go through this. Nigel's scout troop has an allotment, which is one of the best in London. They grow all kinds of vegetables, and even manage strawberries.

I queue for twenty-five minutes. Finally there is only one woman ahead of me.

"Nice bit of rabbit, Mrs. Wilson?"

"Ta very much, Mr. Billy. A bit of liver'd be nice. My son's home on leave this weekend; liver and bacon's his favorite."

"Now that I can't do. There's still a war on, you know. How about a nice bit of tripe? Tripe and onions. Very tasty."

"Tell you the truth, Mr. Billy, I haven't seen an onion in the shops for weeks, and my son isn't a great one for tripe."

A pause. No one dares to offend Mr. Billy. Tripe is actually the stomach of a large bovine animal, like a cow or an ox. I looked it up in the dictionary one day after they served it for school dinners. Thick gray wobbly stuff, with lines on it. No one touched it. *Poor Mrs. Wilson.*

"Seeing it's a special occasion, I'll throw in a soup bone – nice bit of meat on it. One shilling and fourpence, if you please. Next."

"Good afternoon, Mr. Billy. Miss Simmonds was wondering ..." I hesitate.

"What did she have in mind then, a little steak?" Mr. Billy laughs uproariously.

"I don't think I've ever tasted steak, Mr. Billy, and I'm fourteen today."

"What kind of world are we living in, I *ask* you?" This, to the patient woman behind me. "Girls growing up who don't know what a piece of steak tastes like? What are they going to feed their husbands on?"

I try a smile.

The lady behind me says, "Should be on the Music Hall, Mr. Billy. Good as George Formby, you are, any day."

"Flattery will get you everywhere." He rubs his hands over his fat stomach.

I think, *it's disgusting what we have to go through just to eat.*

"Mr. Billy, my aunt was rather hoping for some lamb. She was telling me how, before the war, you had the best spring lamb any-where in West London."

Mr. Billy preens. "Times change, my dear." He goes into the back, returns, and swiftly wraps up a small parcel. "That'll be one shilling and sixpence, please, luv. Regards to your aunt. Sausages for the birthday girl." He winks at me.

I cycle home, whistling all the way, and get in just as Aunt Em is hanging up her gray tweed coat. She's had that coat ever since I've known her. It's not that she can't afford a new one, it's that I'm growing so fast she has to use most of her clothing coupons for me. Mrs. Gibson once said, "An English tweed lasts a lifetime."

Mandy said, "Doesn't it depend how long a lifetime is?" She got told off for being cheeky.

I go into the kitchen and put the kettle on. Aunt Em looks exhausted.

"You okay, Aunt Em?"

"Sophie, I can't tell you how much I dislike that expression." She kisses me absentmindedly. "Happy birthday, darling. How was Mr. Billy?"

"His usual." I remove the string of pinkish gray sausages from the wrapping and swing them round my head like a lasso. "Look what I got. Doesn't it cheer you up?"

"It does, indeed. There is no doubt you know the way to that ogre's heart."

I pour Aunt Em a cup of tea.

"Thank you. I need this. Are you and Mandy on the same shift at the hospital tomorrow?"

"Sister changed her to mornings this week, and I'm on from five till nine in the evening. I rather like those hours, tidying everything up for visitors, and most people in a good mood."

"It's a bit late for you to cycle home by yourself."

"I come straight home, you know that." Mandy and I have been nursing cadets since we were twelve, and it's got us our war service badge in Guides. "Did you have a rotten day, Aunt Em?"

"I did, rather. Jean Mitchell's husband was killed in action. She got the telegram this morning. I wanted to send her home, and she said, 'I'd *prefer* to stay if you don't mind, Miss Simmonds.

You see, there's no one there now.' Her son's just volunteered for the Merchant Navy. Sorry I'm so gloomy. Let me finish this lovely cup of tea and I'll be myself again."

"You've got it." I am given a look.

"Sometimes, Sophie Mandel, I think I'm sharing my home with a member of the American forces. Where do you pick up these expressions? M*m*, something smells delicious. I'll lay the table."

We have two sausages each and fried tomato and triangles of fried bread.

"You should be working for the Ministry of Food, Sophie, not me. You're a wonderful cook."

Aunt Em had made me an eggless birthday cake with white icing, which was a bit runny because you can't get real icing sugar. We're saving the cake until Mandy and Nigel get here.

"Time for presents," says Aunt Em.

There are two this year, instead of one. I open the big one first.

"Aunt Em, oh, I was hoping for this. Thank you a million times!"

It is a beautiful new sketchbook, a bit bigger than last year's. "I don't know how you do it."

"This is the last one, Sophie. I bought six in 1939, when it looked as if there might be a shortage. Now open your other gift."

"What a beautiful velvet box." I lift the lid. "Aunt Em, is it an identity bracelet? I've always wanted one of those! It looks like real gold. It's got a charm on it." I falter. It isn't a charm, not exactly, nor a bracelet. Aunt Em has given me a gold necklace and on it is a Jewish star, a Star of David.

"Let me fasten it for you, Sophie."

I go into the hall to look in the mirror.

I hate wearing anything round my neck. It's choking me. Why would Aunt Em give me this? Religion isn't part of our lives.

Aunt Em says, "Last week during my lunch-hour walk, I passed by my favorite antique shop – the tiny one almost hidden away in the mews. I bought my little rose-colored carriage lamp there before the war. On an impulse, I went in. The owner remembered me. He was pricing some estate jewelry on the counter. I decided to buy this piece. He told me it was very old – of Persian design. I wondered who it had belonged to."

"Thank you, Aunt Em. It's lovely. I'll keep it for special occasions."

There is a familiar knock at the door.

"That'll be Nigel and Mandy." I'm relieved to get away. I put the necklace back in the box, and into my pocket.

"Happy birthday, Sophie." Mandy hugs me.

Nigel pushes a big tin into my hand. "Many happy returns."

"What is it?"

"Open it. It's from all of us," Mandy says.

"Toffee. I don't believe it! However did you . . .?"

"We made it, didn't we, Nigel? It's from one of the Ministries' Christmas recipes. It's called honeycomb toffee."

"Carrot-based," Nigel says solemnly.

"Liar. Don't listen to him, Soph. We saved our sugar ration, and Mum gave us the syrup and voilà!"

For the rest of the evening we play Monopoly and eat toffee and almost finish the birthday cake. "You must take the last piece home for your mother. Please thank her for the syrup," I remind Mandy.

After they leave, Aunt Em says, "I'll do the dishes. You've done more than your fair share, getting supper and facing Mr. Billy."

"Good night, Aunt Em. You do spoil me. It's been a wonderful birthday."

· 5 ·

All evening I'd been conscious of the box in my pocket. I'm not sure why I was in such a hurry to put the necklace out of sight.

I wish I hadn't said I'd been hoping for an identity bracelet. In a way, it is. In Europe Jews wear a star to identify who they are. Like us carrying identity cards to prove we're entitled to a ration book. It's not the same, though. Hitler hates the Jews more than all his other enemies.

I'm sure Mother said once that I'd been christened. She'd have told Aunt Em those kinds of things, seeing they were pen friends. Aunt Em's a Quaker and doesn't believe in organized religion. I go to midnight mass at Christmas with the Gibsons, and Aunt Em stays home and greets us with cocoa after the service.

The little velvet box fits into one of the desk's cubbyholes. I can't think of a special occasion when I'd wear it.

I breathe in the special newness of my sketchbook. At school we use exercise books that have thin yellowish utility paper. Hopeless for real drawing. This paper is thick and made specially for sketching.

Five years ago, I, Sophie Mandel, of 16, Great Tichfield Street, London WC1, made an unbreakable rule: THE OLD SKETCHBOOK MUST BE COMPLETED BEFORE I AM ALLOWED TO BEGIN DRAWING IN THE NEW ONE.

Two pages left. I decide to let my pencil improvise, the way a musician does.

Twenty minutes later, I look at my drawing. It's of a rather grand brick building. I've shaded the bricks gray, but they should be old rose. There's an arched doorway of thick heavy wood, not the kind that would break easily. Above the arch is a stone tablet inscribed with ancient writing. The windows are high and narrow, like church windows. There's a small courtyard enclosed by a low stone wall. Wrought-iron gates in the center are ornamental. The gates are open. In the middle of each one is a circle and a perfect six-point star. . . .

Papa comes home early. He holds a handkerchief to his face.

"Are you hurt, Papa?" Zoffie asks.

"Your papa was careless; he fell out of a tree. Put your hand in my pocket, Zoffie."

The little girl finds a fir cone. "Mm, it smells the way you do when you come home from work – like pine trees. Thank you, Papa."

"Where is Mama?"

"Mama works late on Fridays, Papa."

Sometimes on Saturday mornings, Zoffie goes to the shop to help her mama. She picks up pins that are scattered on the floor of the workroom, where Mama does alterations for rich ladies. Mama shortens sleeves and lengthens hems and always talks with a pin between her teeth. They play a game – will Mama drop the pin?

Papa says, "Let's go for a little walk. Put your coat and hat on; it's cold for November."

Zoffie thinks it is a very long walk. They stop outside a big stone house and pass through some pretty gates. There is a side door, and they go in. Papa keeps his hat on. They cross a large hall and stand at the back of a high-ceilinged room filled with people.

Zoffie sees many candles flickering. On a small balcony, some little girls sit with their mothers. A man sings a song that makes Zoffie want to cry. The men wear long white scarves embroidered with silver and gold. They sway back and forth and sing words that Zoffie doesn't understand.

Papa bows to a man with a long beard; he stares at them.

Papa holds the girl's hand tight. "Time to go," he whispers. Outside it's dark. "Let's hurry, Mama will have supper waiting."

Footsteps behind them. They come closer. Papa's breath is loud and fast.

"Will it snow, Papa?" He doesn't answer.

"Jacob, wait," a voice calls out behind them.

They stop. Papa turns round slowly, gently nudging Zoffie so she stands in front of him. Papa puts his hands on her shoulders.

"A beautiful child, Jacob. It is good to see you once more. We must leave for Poland next week."

Papa puts out a hand. The old man covers it with both of his own. Then he touches Zoffie's cheek with one finger, turns, and goes back toward the stone house.

"Papa, is that St. Nicholas?"

"Can you keep a secret?" he asks.

Zoffie nods.

"That is your grandfather. My father. He is going away. I wanted him to see you. A long time ago, we had a disagreement."

"Were you angry with him, Papa?"

"We were angry with each other."

"What is the palace called, Papa?"

"It is not a palace, Zoffie. It is a place where Jews go to pray. It is called a synagogue. Now hurry, and remember it's a secret."

Mother is waiting for us. "Zoffie, your cheeks are cold like little winter apples." She puts the back of her hand against my cheek, where Grandfather's finger had touched it. "Quickly wash your hands for supper."

Zoffie hears Mama say, "Jacob, your face is bruised."

"I got in the way of a small demonstration. It is nothing for you to worry about."

"Where were you tonight? I asked you not to go out late. It's too dangerous."

Zoffie sees Papa put his arms round Mama. "A little walk, that's all, Liebchen. Even a Jew must have exercise."

"Only a crazy Jew goes out on a Friday night. Promise me to be more careful. Go to work, come home. Stay home with us."

"I promise."

For supper there are sausages and fried potatoes. Zoffie eats two sausages.

. 6 . .

Victory in Europe. V-E Day. Thursday, May 8, 1945. At last it's official: Victory in Europe.

"We want the king. We want the king."

Jammed amongst the crowd of thousands, we wait outside a floodlit Buckingham Palace for the Royal Family to appear. Every time the palace curtains move, the chants get louder. Mandy digs her fingers into my arm with excitement.

At last the French windows open. The moment we've been waiting for. The king in naval uniform, Her Majesty Queen Elizabeth smiling radiantly, and the princesses standing beside their parents.

"They're waving at us," Mandy screams. "Doesn't Princess Margaret look beautiful? She's exactly my age. Oh, I love that little blue hat."

"Don't you wish we'd been old enough to join up, Mandy? I could have been a war artist."

"Can't hear you!" Mandy shouts in my ear.

"Good old Winnie," yells the crowd as Prime Minister Winston Churchill comes out on the balcony. He raises his arm and holds up his fingers in the Victory sign, puffing away at his fat cigar.

We must have stood and cheered for hours, and then, when finally the balcony's empty again, we follow the crowd into the gardens of Buckingham Palace, where the lake shimmers with the reflection of a thousand lights, and a bonfire sparks into the warm May night.

Later, carried along by the crowd surging down the wide avenue of Pall Mall and into Trafalgar Square, we're hugged and kissed, jostled and squeezed.

"This is the most exciting night of our whole lives. Hang on to me, Sophie, so we don't get separated." Mandy's voice is beginning to sound hoarse.

We push our way up the steps of the Portrait Gallery. All you can see for miles are people. It's as if the whole of London is standing at the feet of Nelson's Column.

Words can't begin to describe it. *I need to draw it.*

Buildings dark for so long, now bathed in light. Colored streamers, bunting, and flags everywhere. The splash of fountains, and girls pulling up their skirts and wading into the water. A sailor climbs up a lamppost waving his cap at a bobby, who wants him to get down. Couples sit entwined on the massive dark stone lions. Men and women in uniform from around the world: Poles, Americans, Czechs, Canadians, and the forces of the Free French. Our own Tommies and two Highlanders in kilts blowing bagpipes.

I clutch the pencil stub in my pocket, willing myself not to forget a single thing.

A snaking line of dancers follows a makeshift band and struggles to keep in time to the conga beat. We run down to join in, matching our steps and voices with the conga line: "I came, I saw, I conga." On the Thames behind us, ships hoot and blow Victory whistles, drowning us out. The line makes it to Piccadilly Circus before it disperses into smaller groups.

We collapse out of breath. "I've got to take my shoes off," Mandy gasps. We find a small space on the crowded steps below the statue of the little winged archer. Eros is still partly boarded up, but his wings gleam.

"This morning, church bells woke me up. I jumped out of bed in a panic, thinking we'd been invaded, and then I remembered it's V-E Day," I say. "Can you remember the sound of church bells?"

Mandy shakes her head. "I'll miss it, you know," she confesses.

"Miss what?"

"The war. I don't mean the killing and the bombs or my dad going to war, but the good part."

"Amanda Gibson, there is no good part. I know what you mean, though. The excitement and us being part of something so huge, and the danger."

Mandy says, "I don't know how to live in peacetime. None of us knows."

"Well, the grown-ups will have to work it out." Then I look up and see a group of nurses, quite young – first year's. One of them wears her cap rakishly over one ear. She looks straight at me. Pauses, stares, and looks back after her group has moved on.

People say if you sit in Piccadilly Circus long enough, you're bound to see someone you know. *I know the face, but from where?*

"Sophie, you're as white as a sheet. What's the matter?"

"Nothing. Ghosts."

"What?"

"I saw someone I thought I knew."

"For a minute you looked as if you were going to faint. Are you hungry?" Mandy's worried.

"How could I possibly be hungry after all the food at the celebration tea? I'm going to dream about that trifle. Sponge fingers and jelly and fruit and custard and cream. Where on earth did they get it all? I must have eaten four salmon sandwiches."

"I thought Nigel was going to finish the sausage rolls by himself. I felt quite proud of Mum's Victory cake. Real icing and eggs," Mandy says. "The whole idea of street parties is amazing. It's as if every mother in the land had put something special away just for today. I can't think where your Aunt Em's been hiding that tin of pineapple. Under the bed, where you wouldn't find it." Mandy laughs. "Mum said it was for us, the children, because we've had to go without for so long. There was plenty for everyone in the street. Old Mrs. Benson ate more than anyone, did you notice?"

"Aunt Em thinks rationing will go on and on. She said, 'We'll have to feed Europe now.' Let's go home." We both yawn.

"Pull me up, Sophie."

"Come on, then. Bus or tube?"

"Buses aren't running, luv," a soldier volunteers cheerfully.

"Tube's quicker anyway." I link arms with Mandy.

The queue goes all the way down the steps. The woman in front of us says to her husband, "Reminds me of the Blitz, waiting for a place to sleep on the platform. All those strangers camped out between white chalk marks, huddled together hoping there wouldn't be a direct hit. People coming off the trains and stepping over us to get home. Thank God it's over."

When we reach Baker Street, Mandy leans against a lamppost. "Lovely lovely light," she says. "Do you think we can find our street? I only know the way in the dark." She smiles blissfully up at the brightness.

"Time to go home, Mandy. Good night."

"Night, Sophie."

· 7 ·

When I get in, Aunt Em is sitting by the open window. She'd made tea. "You're wearing your pearls, and your best blouse. You do look nice," I say.

"Thank you, dear. Did you have a lovely time?"

"I don't think I'll ever forget it. Is peace always going to be like this? Like Brighton Pier? It never got dark tonight. Bonfires and searchlights and floodlights and lamplight. I think every light-bulb in London must be on."

"Goodness, I hope not. What a waste of energy."

"How was your party, Aunt Em? Did you have a splendid celebration?"

"It was very festive. We all toasted the king after his speech with prewar sherry, and then the six of us did full justice to Mrs. Mallory's dinner. Corned beef carved in very thin slices, and a lovely salad with cucumber and radishes and tomatoes and new potatoes. Mr. Mallory is a wonderful gardener. After *all* that, we had rhubarb pie with cream from the top of the milk. How I could eat so much after our lovely Victory tea, I don't know."

"It sounds very sumptuous. Aunt Em, do you believe in ghosts?" I ask.

"I don't think so," she says thoughtfully. "I do think there are times when something makes us remember the past very strongly, and we may think we see or sense someone from that time. Tonight there were ghosts with us in the dining room. We talked about that other war, and Armistice Day in 1918. We thought then that peace would last forever."

"It will this time, Aunt Em, you'll see." I want to comfort her.

"I can't help thinking of all the men and women who will never come home. One of the guests tonight has a son in a prison camp in the Far East. He was captured in Malaya in 1941. We've still got that war to finish," Aunt Em says.

The phone rings. "Whoever can be calling at this hour? It's past eleven." Aunt Em picks up the receiver.

"If it's work, say no. Tomorrow's an official holiday," I whisper.

"Gerald, what a nice surprise. Good. Yes, we're fine. It *is* an exciting night. . . . Thank you. We'll try to come down soon. Love to Winifred. Yes. Good-bye, Gerald."

I say, "*Love* to Aunt Winifred? We're going to *see* them?" I pull a face and get one of Aunt Em's looks. Then she gives in and smiles.

"I'll concede, Sophie, that Aunt Winifred is not the easiest person to get along with. I've never quite forgiven her for her attitude when I told her you were coming to stay with me – that air of superiority she had as she said, 'Well, really, Margaret. I find that rather eccentric. You know nothing about bringing up children. People will think it very odd – a single woman with a child.'"

"I think you managed beautifully, Aunt Em."

"Thank you. Oh dear, the first time you met Aunt Winifred, you were so naughty. It was early 1939. You'd been here about two months. I think you must have taken an instant dislike to Winifred."

"Good instincts?" I ask.

"Sophie!"

"Well, Aunt Em, she was looking me over as though I were a dog she was going to buy."

"You can't possibly remember that. You weren't even eight years old."

"I do."

"Winifred was upset because she'd heard that if there was going to be a war, she'd have to take in evacuees. It was actually quite funny. She said, 'I really don't think it's fair. They could send me *anyone*. Slum children, with *things* in their hair. Gerald, you're a solicitor. Do something.'

"Gerald said, 'I don't think that argument will carry any weight with the authorities who are trying to protect the nation's children.'

"She was very put out that Gerald disagreed with her."

"Then Aunt Winifred asked me if I liked dolls," I say.

"Quite right. She announced: 'I've got the perfect solution. I mean, Sophie looks like a dear clean little girl. I can tell the authorities that my sister-in-law and her ward will be using the guest room. After all, Margaret, it would be merely a temporary arrangement, wouldn't it? Should danger arise.'

"It was then that you surprised me. I didn't even know you had such an extensive vocabulary, or could understand so much English!

"'I do not like dolls,' you said. 'I have the tummy ache very often. I cannot sleep. I cry all the time.' Such fibs. You never, well hardly ever, cried. You slept ten hours at least every night, and to the best of my knowledge, had a cast-iron stomach."

"Well, mostly I do," I say.

"I was both proud and ashamed of you. Uncle Gerald, who is surprisingly perceptive, said, 'Sophie seems to have settled the question. We'd better get along, my dear. Two and a half hours' drive, at least. Thanks for tea, Margaret.'"

"Uncle Gerald gave me a shilling when they left."

"More than you deserved, young lady."

"You would have been bored with a perfect child, Aunt Em."

"No danger of that. Good night, darling. Don't stay up drawing too late."

"How did you know I was going to?"

"Like my brother, I'm quite perceptive. I'll come and tuck you up soon."

"Good. I don't think Aunt Winifred has tucked anyone up in her entire life."

"Sophie, Gerald is my only brother. Let's make an effort." I kiss the top of her head and say okay and run!

One of the things I can't bear about Aunt Winifred is that she's always reminding me that I don't belong here. She makes me feel "temporary." I'm not, I *do* belong here. It's my home.

Upstairs I rough in some of the sights: the statue of Eros, the crowds, the face of the girl who had stared at me. No good, I can't do anything justice – I'm too tired. My hair on the pillow smells of smoke from the bonfire in the palace gardens. I close my eyes. . . .

Mama lets Zoffie carry the string bag with apples home from the evening market. It's cold. Zoffie wears her new red hat and mittens. The street lamps are lit; people hurry home.

Mama rolls pastry and slices apples. "*Apfel kuchen für Papa.*" Very carefully Zoffie layers the apple slices, then Mama gives her a handful of raisins to sprinkle over them.

"When is Papa coming home?" Zoffie asks.

"Soon."

The apple pie is ready; it had cooled. Mama and Zoffie wait. Then they eat supper.

A soft tap and a voice at the door. "Frau Mandel, let me in." It is Frau Wiege from upstairs. "There is burning, looting in the streets." She whispers something, and goes out hurriedly. Mama locks the door.

"What is burning, Mama?"

"Leaves, grass."

"The leaves are finished, Mama, it's winter."

"And some are left. It's your bedtime."

"Mama, when is . . .?"

"No more questions, Zoffie."

There are noises in the night: breaking glass, shouting and laughing, tires screeching in the street outside their apartment. The air is full of smoke.

In the morning, Mama says, "No school today. You can come to work with me."

Mama's shop is beautiful, not like next door. The glass is smashed there. Herr Eckstein is scrubbing the pavement. He does not look at them.

Mama hurries Zoffie into the back room. She begins her search for pins. When the lady who owns the shop comes in, Zoffie hides under the table.

"Good morning, Frau Mandel. I am sorry to bring you bad news. You are a good worker, but there have been changes. I am sure you understand. You need not finish out the week. Here. . . ." She gives Zoffie's mama an envelope.

Papa does not come home again that night.

Next day, very early, they hear Papa's key in the door.

"The Gestapo let me go – this time. I am a Jew with an Aryan wife. My employer says the work I do is 'essential'; it can be done only by someone like me."

"For how long is gardening essential?" Mama asks, and pours Papa his coffee. She does not smile.

"I have not eaten since the ninth."

"Two days?" Mama cuts more bread. "Later we'll talk. Not now."

"Zoffie," Papa says, when he finishes breakfast. "What shall I draw for you?"

"A garden. Papa, we baked you an apple pie. Where were you?"

"In a garden like the one I'm drawing for you. It's called a maze – a labyrinth."

"Where are the flowers? Why are the paths going round and round in circles?"

"It is a crazy garden – a kind of puzzle. People go into the labyrinth. Some stay and go round and round forever. Some are lucky and find the way out."

"Let me draw, too." Zoffie draws labyrinths for the rest of the day.

That night I dream of Nazi soldiers chasing a girl round and round a garden. They follow her into a labyrinth. Someone starts a fire.

I wake up and call out a name – *Marianne*.

I hardly ever remember my dreams, and I haven't seen Marianne in almost seven years.

. 8 .

We'd eaten our sandwiches and lay in the long, sweet-smelling grass on top of Parliament Hill. The three of us had cycled all the way to Hampstead Heath, and I was almost asleep.

Mandy, who's incapable of staying still for more than one minute, tickles my neck with a blade of grass. "Let's do something."

Nigel mumbles, "Too hot."

"You know what she's like. We may as well give in graciously. I'll agree to anything as long as I don't have to move," I say.

"How about best thing/worst thing?" Mandy says.

"No point doing best thing because we're bound to say it's V-E Day."

"Worst thing's more fun," says Nigel.

"It's got to be the worst thing we've ever done that we've not told each other before," I say. "One minute thinking time. Go."

"I'll start," Nigel says. "I was very young, you understand . . ."

"Oh, get on with it, twin . . ."

"I'd got a new penknife for cubs and Mike Rivers –"

"Mike – the worst boy in the street – the one Dad said you weren't supposed to play with?" Mandy exclaims.

"I'm not sure that this story's going to be suitable for our delicate sensibilities," I add.

"Do you want me to tell you or not?" Nigel says severely.

"Mike got hold of a piece of alder wood, which is easy to carve. I said, 'Let's make a pipe.' I carved the bowl, scooping out the wood to make a little cup. Then we cut down a piece of garden cane, made a notch in the side of the bowl, and twisted the cane into it. We found some oak leaves and stuffed the pipe and lit it. We had a really good smoke, except for the coughing."

"That's it?" I say. "Every little boy in the country smokes at some time, and that's the worst thing you ever did? Pathetic!"

"I expected something awful. It's not good enough. I hoped for better from my twin," Mandy says.

"Put it this way," says Nigel, trying to reestablish his authority, "that's all I'm prepared to confess at this time."

Mandy sticks her tongue out at Nigel and says, "I'll go next. When we were evacuated and I was at Mrs. Kingsley's in Kent, she sent me out one Saturday morning for a loaf of bread. She gave me two shillings and told me not to lose the change. It was early; the loaf was still warm – it had just come out of the oven. I was starving, as usual. The bread smelled so good, I thought, 'If I pick off a tiny bit of the crust, no one will notice.' I broke off a tiny piece, and it tasted wonderful. I still don't know how it happened, but next time I looked, I'd eaten half the loaf.

"I started to cry. I didn't know what to do. I wanted to go and tell Nigel. Then I had an inspiration: 'If I finish all the bread, I can tell her I lost the money. Anyone can fall down and lose two shillings.' I convinced myself that I'd fallen on the path down to the village, scraped my knee, and seen the coin roll away before I could catch it. I even rubbed dirt on my knee. So I went back and said, 'I'm very very sorry Mrs. Kingsley, I lost the money. I'll write Mummy and she'll send you some more.'

"She gave me a spanking and sent me up to bed for the rest of the day. She didn't give me anything, not even a drink. I could smell her cooking tea, something with fried onions."

"Old witch," Nigel mutters. I have a feeling if he'd been with Mike Rivers, he'd have said something a lot worse.

"What's the verdict?" Mandy asks.

"She was an awful woman and she ill-treated you, so the lie was out of fear," I comment.

"Still, it was a lie and stealing. In fact, a premeditated act," Nigel says.

We consult. "The punishment is, you have to write a letter to her, explaining what you did, and enclose a postal order for the amount you stole, and tell her how she drove you to it," I say.

"By the way, what *did* you do with the change?" Nigel asks.

"I threw it away, so the lie would only be a little fib. I love the punishment. It'll get rid of my guilt."

"Mandy," I say, "you can't mean that. I mean, about feeling guilty. She stole. The government and your mother paid her to take care of you and she starved you. Actually, for a child of eight, I think it was rather a brilliant way out of the situation.

"Now I'll tell you my evil deed. It happened about three years ago. Miss Merton was teaching us gym. She was at least sixty even then because all the young teachers had been called up for the war effort. I hated going to class and that morning I'd forgotten to bring my gym blouse. She told me I'd have to participate in my vest and knickers. So I told her I hadn't brought my blouse because I had an awful headache and a stomachache and I was hoping she'd excuse me. She said I'd better go home and bring her a note next day.

"I couldn't believe my luck, and decided I'd do some sketching. There'd been a raid the night before and I thought, 'If London keeps getting bombed, there'll be no record of any of the great buildings left.'

"I started close to the school. First I drew Nash Crescent, that lovely curve of houses near Albany Street. Then I cycled to the Royal Academy of Music. I thought I'd have time to draw the BBC before lunch too. I'd just got the outline right when I felt a tap on my shoulder. A policeman was looking down at me. 'I'll take care of that, Miss,' he said, and removed my sketchbook and began to leaf through it.

"'It's all right,' I explained, 'I've got permission to be absent from school.' I thought Miss Merton had changed her mind and sent a policeman to find me, and I'd be punished for missing school.

"'Fond of drawing important landmarks, are you?' he said. 'I think you'd better come along to the station, young lady, and tell the sergeant about what you've been up to.'

"I had to wheel my bike while he walked beside me. I couldn't think what all the fuss was about. It's not as if I'd been stealing, or anything like that. He took me into the sergeant's office. I was allowed to sit down while they conferred. I thought I'd better apologize, so I did and said I'd never do it again.

"The sergeant looked at my sketches and asked, 'Who put you up to this?'

"I got confused at the question, so I told him the truth – that I'd forgotten to bring my gym blouse to change into, and that I hated gym anyway, had pleaded a headache, and was sent home.

"He demanded my name and wrote it down. Then he wanted to know my age and place of birth. The looks on their faces when I said Berlin, Germany made me feel like a criminal. He wanted to know if I lived with my parents. I was a bit frightened by then, so I said I was an orphan, and I lived with my guardian, who worked at the Ministry of Food.

"'Who told you to tell this story if you're caught?' he asked, and he and the constable kept giving each other meaningful looks. Honestly, I didn't know what he was talking about. I mean it's not as though I'd deliberately planned to forget my gym blouse.

"Then he said they'd check my statements, and my drawings were confiscated. I was just going to ask him not to do that

because they were important, when he pointed his finger at me –
you know the way they always show on the posters when they
issue a warning to the public about something. He said that the
enemy was everywhere, and I wouldn't be the first child who'd
been recruited as a spy. He said any drawing or photograph that
might give information to the enemy was a major offence. 'I want
the truth,' he said. He was really stern and I had visions of being
locked up for years. I wondered when they were going to take my
fingerprints.

"I said, 'Please, Sir, I am telling you the truth: I'm not a spy.
I'm a refugee from the Nazis. Drawing's my hobby.' I promised
him I'd never miss gym again, even if I had to take it in my vest
and knickers. I prayed they'd believe me."

Nigel's shoulder's shook with laughter and Mandy was rolling
on the grass and howling. A woman walking her dog made a wide
berth round us. "Hooligans," we heard her say.

"I think it was the vest part that convinced them. The
sergeant told the constable to escort me back to school. 'If you
were a few years older, young lady, you would be interned as an
enemy alien. As it is, you may well be taken into protective
custody. I hope I have made myself clear?'

"I didn't dare speak after that, and just nodded.

"The constable took me right inside the school and made sure
I went into the office. I told the secretary that I hadn't felt well
and had permission to go home, but that I now felt very much
better, and please would she tell Miss Merton that I was back for

my lessons. Can you imagine if I had to ask Aunt Em for a note?"

"Old Miss Merton, who's almost senile?" Mandy says, wobbling her chin in imitation of the gym teacher.

"This is definitely the worst thing I've ever heard you do, Sophie," Nigel says. "I can see the sergeant's point. You *could* have been passing on information."

Nigel and Mandy whisper for a few minutes. "We think a suitable punishment would be to give up your sweet ration for a month, then buy some chocolate for Miss Merton, and write a note telling her how much you appreciate all she's done for the school, and how you've always loved her lessons."

"That would be another lie, and awfully cruel," I say.

"No appeals, not even on the grounds of being a foreigner who didn't know any better."

The game is almost turning into something unpleasant. For a moment, Nigel has seen me not as his best friend, but as an alien – a foreigner. *Is this what peace is going to be like?*

Mrs. Gibson is cooking spam fritters for supper, with mashed potatoes and runner beans from their garden. There is a lovely smell of baked apples.

"Nigel's doing dishes tonight, Mum," Mandy says, looking meaningfully at her brother. "He offered, didn't you, twin?"

Mrs. Gibson is just pouring the last of the custard over Mandy's helping of baked apple, when a voice booms from the hall: "Anyone home?"

"Dad!" The three of them fly out of the kitchen and I just

manage to save the jug from tipping over. I'm mopping up a few drops of custard that have dripped onto the table when Mr. Gibson, or rather Corporal Gibson of His Majesty's Transit Corps, puts his kit bag down in the corner.

"Hello, young Sophie, you've grown again. How's your aunt?"

"Fine, Sir. Thank you. It's awfully good to see you."

"Sit down, Dan. I'll make you some bacon and eggs, all right?" asks Mrs. Gibson.

"Perfect, luv. Good to stretch my legs under my own kitchen table. Seven days' leave. Surprised you, didn't I?"

Mandy stands behind his chair and twines her arms round his neck. Mrs. Gibson is putting what looks like a month's ration of bacon into the pan.

"Thank you very much for the delicious supper, Mrs. Gibson. I'd better get on home. Good night, Mr. Gibson."

Nigel follows me into the hall. "It was a great day, Soph. See you at the dance on Friday."

Everything's all right again.

It takes me only five minutes to cycle home from the Gibsons'. Their happiness at being together again reminds me how few relatives I've got. For years there's been only Aunt Em. Her parents died in the influenza epidemic of 1919, or I'd have "adopted" grandparents the way Aunt Em's my "adopted" aunt.

How did she get through such an awful time – losing her parents, her brother, and her fiancé? She must have loved him an awful lot to have never got married.

53

Supposing it wasn't a lie that time I told the police I was an orphan? If it *was* true, would Aunt Em adopt me? Not that I *want* to be an orphan. I'm not wishing away my parents, or anything. They're safe. Parents don't die without their children finding out. I'd *know* something like that.

At birthdays and Christmas, Aunt Em always says she's certain my parents are thinking of me, that once the war's over letters will start arriving.

At breakfast this morning, Aunt Em reminded me again that it won't be long before we hear from Mama and Papa. She said if there's too much of a delay, she'd get in touch with the Red Cross. I was hoping we could talk about what would happen when letters do start arriving. *Will Aunt Em and I go on as before?* When you've lived in a place more than half your life, it's pretty devastating to think about changing.

Aunt Em seems to avoid talking about the subject, and I don't want to make an issue of it. *I'm a coward.*

· 9 ·

"Wasn't it heaven getting two days off in the middle of the week, Sophie? Tomorrow's the Victory dance. Have you got your costume ready?"

Mandy and I are in the school cafeteria, at lunchtime on Thursday.

"Mum's helping me finish off a witch's cloak from the upstairs blackout curtains. She says she's only too pleased to get rid of them! I still need a hat, though."

"I requisitioned a piece of cardboard from the salvage box. Thought the war effort could spare it. I'll make it into a coned hat for you, and we can paste stars and symbols on it."

"Thanks, Sophie. How about your costume?"

"Mine's easy. I'll go as an Impressionist artist – you know, wearing a beret. Aunt Em found a sort of Russian-looking smock in amongst the Red Cross things in the spare room. It's got very wide sleeves. I'll wear her spotted scarf tied in a floppy bow round my neck. That should do. I've got a pair of black woolen stockings too. I may die of heatstroke, though. Which reminds me, what are you wearing under your cloak?"

"Mum's come to the rescue again. She got a blue full-length slip; if I knot the shoulder straps it'll fit me. Bother, there's the bell. Biology, next. If Miss Carter asks me to dissect an earthworm, I shall refuse on the grounds of animal rights," Mandy declares.

"I think she looks a bit wormy herself," I add.

On Friday night, we get to the dance at 7:30 and the room is already packed.

"Great decorations, Sophie," Mandy says.

"I can only take half the credit – Nigel did a lot of ladder-climbing too."

The kitchen committee has put colored cotton strips of red, white, and blue bunting to cover the tables, and there are jugs of homemade lemonade, as well as an urn of tea and platters of sandwiches, with little flags stuck into the bread: meat paste, fish paste, and Marmite. There are several plates of biscuits too.

We'd painted the lightbulbs in different colors – green, red, and blue – so the old rec room would be romantically transformed.

Nigel looks very dashing as a pirate with a patch over his eye. I am a bit concerned about his feet, stuck in huge Wellington boots. Mandy says other than the waltz, not too much progress has been made with the dancing lessons.

We all wear numbers pinned to our backs so that the prize committee can judge our costumes more easily as we dance.

The M.C. (who is Reverend Peter's curate) announces a general "Excuse Me" dance. Vera Lynn's voice drifts enticingly through the loudspeaker.

Mandy is dancing with Reverend Peter at the far end of the room, and Simon and I circle slowly under the blue lights.

Nigel is talking to Stanley, a newcomer. I don't like him – he's already made some nasty comments about people and then laughed them off as a joke. I notice that Stanley's wearing jodhpurs and riding boots, and carrying a crop.

Nigel comes over and takes my hand. Simon shrugs his shoulders in exaggerated disappointment. Everyone is having fun.

Stanley says loudly, over the music, "Bit soon to be fraternizing with the enemy, isn't it? Time to go home, Fräulein."

Nigel's face is so white, every one of his freckles stands out. He lets go of my hand, walks over to Stanley, grabs his arm, and pushes him out of the back door. "Wait for me," he says over his shoulder.

Someone cranks up the gramophone. Simon comes over to me, and we finish the dance. Luckily it's almost over.

When I get outside, Mandy is already there. The twins have a sort of built-in radar about each other. Mandy is staunching a stream of blood from Nigel's nose. Stanley is on his hands and knees, shaking his head. He stands up, and I see he has a black eye.

Mandy is furious. "You're a fine pair," she says. "Look at you. This is supposed to be a dance celebrating Victory, not the start of a new war."

Reverend Peter comes out to join us. "I have no idea what this is about, however, I suggest you shake hands and then come into the kitchen for repairs. There should be some ice there," he says.

Stanley mumbles something and walks off.

I pick up the riding crop. I feel like hurling it after him. Instead I hand it to Reverend Peter.

"Thank you, Sophie. You know where I am if you need me."

Nigel speaks for the first time. "Thanks, Mandy. I think the bleeding's stopped." He shoves the bloody handkerchief in his pocket.

"I'll go back in, then. Hurry up or you'll be too late for the judging." Mandy goes back in to the dance.

"Sorry, Nigel." I say.

"For what?"

"You know." *Does he expect me to say that I am the cause of the fight because of where I've been born?*

Nigel leans against the wall of the alley.

A thin black kitten twines its body round my legs and begins to scratch my stockings. "Ow." I pick up the kitten and stroke its fur. "Are you hungry?" The kitten begins to purr. "Nigel, you don't have to fight my battles. I've been called names before."

Nigel says, "Remember when you and Mandy were being bullied by that gang in the village? Didn't I sort it out? No one's going to get away with calling you names while I'm around. If that Stanley what's-his-name so much as looks your way again, you let me know."

"I told you. I don't want anyone to fight about me. People like Stanley aren't worth it." I smile at him. I don't want him to think he's not appreciated. "Now, let's take this poor starving animal inside and feed it."

"Okay." Nigel leans forward and strokes the cat's ears. His head is very close to mine; his hair brushes my cheek.

I smile. This is almost as romantic as the shipboard scene when Paul Henreid and Bette Davis share a cigarette in *Now Voyager*.

"What's the joke about?" Nigel asks, as we go back inside.

"I was actually thinking about smoking."

"Smoking! I didn't know you smoked, Sophie."

"I don't."

Mandy wins first prize for her witch costume, and Nigel walks me home.

If I was asked to say the best thing about this evening, it would have to be the touch of Nigel's hair on my face. The worst thing – that horrible Stanley. How dare he? *Time to go home, Fräulein.*

I am home. This is my home and no one's going to say or do anything to change that.

· IO ·

I'm always early for my volunteering at the hospital – partly because of what Sister would say if I weren't punctual, but mostly because I enjoy it more than anything I do for the war effort. Peace effort, I suppose I should say now, even though the war in the Far East is still on.

A hospital's a world of its own, quite different from what goes on outside. I should think working here is a bit like being in the forces. I'm on the lowest rung, like a recruit – someone who's just joined up – but I feel useful.

The porter recognizes me now. "Nice day, Miss," or "Looks like rain." Most of the nurses seem pleased to have an extra pair of hands, and even talk about the patients in front of me as if I belong.

I know that the bandages I've rolled will be used for wounds almost at once. When I arrange a vase of flowers, or plump a pillow, or make up beds with the corners tucked in tightly, I'm doing something useful. Last week I was allowed to sterilize the thermometers. I admit polishing bedpans is not what I enjoy doing most, but Sister-in-charge actually said, "Well done, dear."

For the next five Saturdays, I'm on women's surgical. My favorite is the children's ward. I love the babies; they're not afraid to tell you if something hurts – they scream. Adult patients think they're a nuisance.

I've barely put on my apron when I'm told to wipe all the wheels on the screens that are put round the beds for privacy. When I've done that, it is time to bring in the supper trays. There are twenty-four women on this ward. Poor things, they're having boiled fish tonight – white fish, with lumpy white gravy. You can smell it all the way down the corridor.

I'd changed the water in the flower vases when a voice, with the trace of a foreign accent, says, "Please make sure beds thirteen and seventeen get the first two trays. The women are on salt-free diets."

I look up and say, "Yes, Nurse." Pick up the trays and put them down again, very slowly and carefully. I need to be sure. I say, "Excuse me, Nurse, didn't we see each other on V-E night . . .?"

"The nurse pauses a moment, then says, "Sophie? You can't be Sophie, *my* Sophie."

We hug each other. "Marianne, I've been thinking about you all week."

"You've grown up. I can't believe it. Do you still sleep all the time?" Marianne takes my hands in both of hers and beams.

"Your hair's different and you're not taller than me anymore," I say.

We laugh and hug again. I can feel tears threatening to well up.

The Ward Sister appears. Her snowy cap sits on her gray hair at a precisely correct angle. As I look down, I can almost see my face reflected in her polished black shoes. She crackles starch with each breath.

"What is the meaning of this unseemly display? I would have thought you knew better, Nurse Kohn. This is a surgical ward, not Piccadilly Circus."

We freeze as though posing for a family portrait.

"Your cap is crooked. Straighten it. Pull down your cuffs."

Marianne adjusts her uniform.

"The supper trays are late. I will see you at the end of your shift, Nurse Kohn."

"Yes, Sister. I'm sorry, Sister," Marianne says. I pick up the trays again and overhear Marianne explain: "Sophie is a great friend. I haven't seen her for over seven years. I'd lost her."

And then Sister's reply: "That will do, Nurse. There will be no further emotional outbursts on my ward."

When supper is over, I wipe the trays down before stacking them neatly on the trolleys to take them down to the kitchen. Marianne whisks in to refill a water jug. She whispers urgently, "My half-day's on Wednesday, let's meet. Are you still at school?"

I nod. "We finish at four. I can meet you anywhere."

"Outside Goodge Street tube station – four thirty. I'd better go."

She glides out. No one ever runs in a hospital; it's the first rule they teach us.

I cycle home in a daze. I can't wait to tell Aunt Em that I've found my ghost. There is a car parked outside number sixteen. A Ford. Which of Aunt Em's friends owns a Ford? I know it's not Uncle Gerald's. Unless he's changed his car, and that's pretty unlikely in wartime. I've got to stop thinking "wartime." It isn't anymore, even though we're being told everything's going to be in shorter supply because of the people in Europe, who have a lot less than we do.

"Aunt Em?" I call, as I enter the house.

"I'm in the sitting room, dear."

We don't usually use that room, except for visitors. We're "kitchen people." Aunt Em is sitting in the armchair. A strange man, at least one I haven't seen before, is holding her wrist.

"This is Sophie, Dr. O'Malley."

"How do you do, Sir?"

The doctor drops Aunt Em's wrist, smiles at me, and says, "Good. We'll soon have you back to normal. Hello, Sophie."

"Aunt Em, what happened – did you fall?"

"Your aunt had a little dizzy spell and called the surgery. Very sensible thing to do."

The man in the tweed jacket, with leather patches at the elbows and the lilt in his speech, isn't our lovely Dr. Baines, who'd taken out my tonsils, painfully, a couple of years ago and nursed me through measles and mumps.

"No need to look so worried, young lady. Dr. Baines is taking his first holiday since 1938, and I'm covering for him. Why don't you help your aunt to her room? Meanwhile, if I might use your telephone, Miss Simmonds, I'll phone a prescription through to Boots Chemist. There's one open late on Baker Street."

When we get upstairs Aunt Em says, "I'm all right now, Sophie. Put a clean towel out for Dr. O'Malley. I'll be tucked up in bed before you know it."

I run down as Dr. O'Malley is replacing the receiver. "Now I'll just wash my hands and be off. I've two more calls to make tonight."

"Will Aunt Em be all right?" I force myself to ask. *I have to know.*

The doctor puts his hand on my shoulder for a moment. "Yes," he says. "Now that the war is over, the strain is showing, that's all. People are tired. They haven't had enough to eat, enough rest, or any holidays for six years of war. Worries about family, getting through air raids. Making do month after month. I call it war fatigue.

"All your aunt needs is some 'peace' and a bit of spoiling. I've told her not to go back to work for a few days. Dr. Baines will be back by then. Good night, Sophie."

I put a white cloth on a tray, and two digestive biscuits on a plate beside the cup and saucer. A jug of milk and the small glazed brown teapot for one, which Aunt Em has had for years and years.

Tomorrow I'll pick some lilies of the valley. There's a clump behind the apple tree. I'll put it on her breakfast tray.

I knock on Aunt Em's door. She's lying against her pillows, her eyes closed. I start to tiptoe out again. . . .

"I'm not asleep, Sophie, just resting."

I plump up the pillows, put another one behind her back, and pour her tea.

"How lovely. It's nice to have my own resident nurse. Sit down and tell me about your day." Aunt Em nibbles a biscuit.

"Tomorrow. I have to cycle down to Boots' now for the prescription. Back in a jiffy."

When I get back, Aunt Em is asleep. I put the medicine, a spoon, and a glass of water beside her. On a note I write: WAKE ME IF YOU NEED ME. Underneath I draw a picture of a lady stranded on a mountain calling help.

I leave both doors open. It is almost eleven before I am in bed. I don't feel the least bit sleepy.

I want to think some more about finding Marianne again, to get used to the idea. Keep her to myself a bit longer before telling Aunt Em about a girl I knew for only two days when I was seven – a girl who's so important to me because she took care of me as if she were my older sister.

I open my new sketchbook and begin to draw.

It is the first time I'd been to a station. I draw the train and the smoke belching up into the roof, which is as high as the sky. I draw a woman wearing a scarf over her head, tied like a kerchief.

I draw hands waving handkerchiefs and mouths shouting good-bye.

I draw the little girl looking at steps too big for her to manage.

I draw the inside of the compartment. There are seven children – four girls and three boys. The seats are hard. Wood. *How do I remember that?*

It's as if I'm sitting there again, instead of on my own soft mattress. Sometimes that happens when I draw. It's as if I'm right inside the picture.

I am squeezed in the middle of the row, between Marianne and a girl with long braids. A boy puts my rucksack overhead. . . .

Papa says, "Take Zoffie to your mother. It's our best chance."

Chance. Chance of what? Is she going to her grandmother's?

"What about you?" asks Mama.

"What about me? I'll trust to luck. Go to work, dig my ditches, come home. Wait for what the next day brings."

What luck is Papa waiting for?

"For how long, Jacob? Face the situation. You are safe only if I stay here with you. I want to stay. I will never leave you."

"Take the child to Dresden. Disappear with her."

Disappear?

"Zoffie is half yours. Mother will close the door in our faces."

Zoffie says, "I want to go to Grandpa with the long beard. I don't want to disappear."

Mama is angry. "Now see what you've done."

Papa says, "Bed, Zoffie."

The girl overhears him telling Mama: "He is an old man, by now over the border in Poland, who knows where. We must get the child away somehow."

Zoffie sits up in her bunk and opens her storybook. She shows the pictures of Hansel and Gretel to Käthe. "This is Hansel and this is Gretel. Their cruel stepmother left them alone in the forest. They could not find their way home. The birds ate the breadcrumbs that Hansel dropped on the path to help the children find their way back. Hansel and Gretel walked and walked. They came to a house made of gingerbread and icing sugar. They ate a piece of the door. It was a knob made of chocolate, and it grew right back again.

"A cruel witch lived in the house. She put Hansel in a cage, to fatten him up for a pie. Each day she said, 'Let me feel your finger,' but Gretel had given her brother a twig to push through the bars to trick the old woman. The witch got tired of waiting for Hansel to get fat, and lit a big fire in the black stove. She opened the door to put on more wood, and Gretel pushed her inside. The witch went up in smoke.

"Then Gretel freed her brother and a little bird showed them the way home and they lived happily ever after."

That must be the night her parents decided to send her away to be safe with Aunt Em.

Wednesday's my favorite day of the week because we get a double period of art. Miss Potter, the art teacher, has brought three objects for our still-life project. When she cuts the orange into quarters, we gasp longingly; it's ages since most of us have even seen an orange. Miss Potter says she'll draw lots after class, so four lucky people will each get a piece.

She arranges the orange quarters on a thick blue platter, and places a plain glass tumbler beside it. The light from the window bounces off them so that the glass catches the colors, like a prism.

After a while Miss Potter comes and stands beside me. She doesn't say anything, she doesn't have to. We both know I'm not concentrating today.

The sight and smell of the orange brings back so many memories that I connect with Marianne. My mother had put an orange in the pocket of my dress before we left Berlin. We were given more oranges on the boat, by the sailors, and again when we arrived in England. Marianne had said she couldn't bear the smell of oranges and offered me hers. I remember being too sleepy to keep awake long enough to answer her.

It's a relief when the bell rings.

Mandy and I hurry so as not to be late for library duty, which is supposed to be a privilege. We've been revising all the catalog cards, making sure that every book on the shelves has a matching card and that all the cards are in alphabetical order.

"You're miles away, Sophie," Mandy says. "Is it because of meeting your friend?"

"That's just it. I don't know if she's a friend or some stranger I spent two days of my life with, and I've built it up out of all proportion."

"What does it matter? Either way, you'll have lots to talk about. It sounds rather like being evacuated," Mandy whispers, but not quietly enough. The librarian materializes.

"Girls, you are not here to gossip. Get on with your work, please." She glares at us.

Rather like being evacuated. I suppose it was – not knowing where we were going, or who'd take us in, and saying good-bye to our parents, except that I'd never actually said good-bye.

The difference I hadn't talked about to Mandy was, the Nazis on the train stole or spoiled our things and twisted Käthe's head off.

Mandy mutters, "Stop biting your nails, Sophie. They're just beginning to look decent."

* * *

Four o'clock comes at last. Washing my hands in the cloakroom, I look in the mirror and see my face. I have two bright red blotches on my cheeks. Nerves.

Mandy says, "Put your hat on, take three deep breaths, and calm down. This isn't an exam."

"Suppose she doesn't turn up?"

"Then you'll go home and listen to the radio, or draw, or go for a bike ride, or talk to Aunt Em, or read. Come on, Sophie, pull yourself together, as our 'revered' headmistress would say. Tell you what – why don't I walk to the tube with you? Let's hurry, though. Dad went back to his unit today, so Mum will want cheering up."

On the way to meet Marianne, I try to explain to Mandy. "You see, she's the only person in England who remembers me from before. I'm not complaining or anything – I know I'm lucky – but you've got Nigel and your parents, and two grandmothers and a grandfather, and goodness knows how many uncles and aunts and cousins."

"You've got Aunt Em," Mandy says.

"You know perfectly well she's not really my aunt. Even her name's not real. I started calling her Aunt Em after the aunt in *The Wizard of Oz*."

"Okay, I forgot. You have my permission to be as nervous as you like. Look, is that her? The nurse by the telephone kiosk. She's waving."

"That's her." I wave back. "Come and be introduced."

"Next time. I'll see you tomorrow."

I cross the road to where Marianne's waiting.

· 12 ·

"I'm a bit early. I couldn't wait to see you again," Marianne says, smiling broadly.

"Me, too." We shake hands rather formally, and that makes us laugh, breaking the ice. "I hope you didn't get into too much trouble with Sister."

"She went on a bit about decorum, and setting an example. She's actually quite decent under all that starch. Sophie, I cannot get over how tall you are. What happened to you?"

"I grew. I was fourteen on April 27."

"I was eighteen on May 3. Let's have some tea. There's a Lyon's restaurant round the corner. It's self-serve. Would you like a sticky bun? I'm always starved. The food at the nursing residence is even worse than the patients get."

Marianne insists on paying.

"Before I forget, Aunt Em said please come for tea or supper when you're free. She's longing to meet you."

"Aunt Em?" Marianne looks puzzled. "Who is Aunt Em?"

"My guardian, alias Miss Margaret Simmonds."

"In that case, of course, I'd love to. Is she the lady who fetched you from Liverpool Street Station – the one in the gray coat?"

"That's her. Still wearing that coat."

"She looked very kind. I watched her face when she spoke to you, and the way she held your hand when you left."

"She *is* kind. She and my mother were pen friends for years before the war, and when things got difficult, she wrote and asked Aunt Em to take care of me. The day we left, Mother said I was going on holiday to England."

The men at the table beside ours are smoking. The gray-blue haze swirls behind Marianne's head. I remember the first time I saw her. . . .

Mama says, "Today is a special day, Zoffie. It's the day you are going on holiday to England. Look, you have a new dress to wear, and so has Käthe. Two pretty girls. There is something in the pocket for you."

"Is the orange for me?"

"Yes, to eat on the journey. Stop jumping up and down. You don't want to be late, do you? Let me brush your hair."

"Are you coming on holiday to England too, Mama?"

"No, how could I? Who would look after Papa? You are such a big girl, you can manage on your own. . . ."

"Is that the holiday train, Mama? It's so big. Why are we waiting? I want to go through the gate."

Mama is talking to a woman holding a list. She is blocking our way.

"Please check again. Her name is Zoffie Mandel. She was promised a place."

"Mama, they are closing the little doors on the train. The guard is blowing the whistle. The train will leave without me!"

"No. It won't. Come quickly." Mama pushes me onto the platform. So many children waving. All going away like me. Mama pulls me along. I hold Käthe away from the soldiers and the fierce dogs.

"Run, Zoffie. See, the door is still open. Good girl. Stay with the children." She lifts me up into the compartment.

"Mama?"

Marianne says, "Your mother kissed your hand before she left and asked me to take care of you. You wore a blue dress."

"With white stripes. Mother sewed it for me."

"I thought so. You wore it over a little white blouse with a Peter Pan collar. By the time we got to England, it was gray. Do you remember how we all stood in a line on the platform at Liverpool Street Station? I was trying to scrub your face clean because photographers were taking pictures of us. We were that day's news: the first refugee children to arrive in England on a *Kindertransport* out of Nazi Germany. I wanted us to make a good impression," Marianne says.

"Later, when we were evacuated from Paddington Station, I was sure you'd be on the train, taking care of me like you did before," I say. "For a long time, in the beginning, I waited for you to come and live with Aunt Em and me."

Marianne bites her thumbnail, then puts her hand back in her lap as if someone had slapped it down. "After you left, Sophie, I really missed you. I waited and waited for my name to be called. Finally, when I was the only girl left in the waiting room, Mrs. Abercrombie Jones agreed to take me."

"Was she kind to you, Marianne?"

"I'll be charitable and say she did her best. Aunt Vera had hoped for an older girl, someone the same age you are now, Sophie, whom she could train as a maid. She hadn't the least idea of how homesick I was, or what we'd been through in Germany.

"It wasn't all bad, of course. I wasn't hungry or beaten, and I made a wonderful friend. It was Bridget who got me through those first awful weeks. She helped me make up job applications to find employment for my parents. Imagine two eleven-year-olds going door-to-door with our little bits of paper, soliciting work."

"What happened?"

"My mother did get a job offer. My father was trapped in Czechoslovakia when Hitler marched in, so there wasn't much hope of him getting out.

"I waited for Mutti's letter, which never arrived, to say when she was coming. We missed each other by hours. She actually arrived in London the day after I was evacuated to Wales. The school was closed, Mrs. Abercrombie Jones had shut the house and moved away, so there was no forwarding address for me. I'd just been thrown out of my third billet when she found me, and

by Christmas we were living together. That reminds me, Sophie –
write down your address; I don't want to lose you again."

I scribble my address for her. Marianne gasps, "I can't believe
it. When I lived with Mrs. Abercrombie Jones, I was less than
half an hour's walk away from you. We lived in St. John's Wood,
on Circus Road. Destiny meant us to meet again."

"Absolutely," I say. "Tell me about Bridget – what happened to
her?"

"Bridget's parents sent her to Canada at the beginning of the
war, to live with an uncle in Montreal. She's sailing home as soon
as she can get a berth on a ship. She's done her probationary year
of nursing in Canada. Her father, Dr. O'Malley, is pulling strings
like mad so she gets accepted at the Middlesex. Bridget and I
really want to finish our training together."

"Marianne, does Dr. O'Malley look anything like this?"

I do a quick sketch on the back of the paper Marianne gives
me, roughing in the doctor's shaggy eyebrows and the lines under
his eyes.

"Sophie, are you clairvoyant or something? That's him."

"Your Dr. O'Malley came to our house last week because our
regular doctor is on holiday."

"It's amazing. Not just that you know him, but the way you
draw."

I try to shrug modestly. "Marianne, where is your mother?"

"She's still working for Mrs. Davy. Now that the war's over,
we're hoping to hear news about my father. Waiting's awful,
isn't it?"

75

"Yes. Do you have any other relatives over there?"

Normally I wouldn't ask anything so personal, but this isn't an ordinary conversation. Or an ordinary meeting.

"My Aunt Grethe is safe in Holland. She and Uncle Frank were in Westerbork Concentration Camp. He died there. She's back at home in Amsterdam now. My cousin Ruth, her daughter, lives in Palestine. She's two years older than me. She sailed there on a rickety old boat just before the Nazis overran Holland in 1940. Ruth lives on a kibbutz called Degania. She and her group are making orchards out of the desert."

"Kibb. . . . I've never heard that word before."

"A kibbutz is a farm that belongs to all the people who live and work there. Uncle Frank was always against her going. He thought the work would be too hard for her. He did relent at the last moment, so Ruth was able to leave with his blessing." Marianne stirs her tea.

I remember the pictures of the camps I've seen. Somehow I can't imagine my father being in such a place. *They'll be all right. After all, my mother isn't Jewish.*

Marianne looks up at me. "My grandparents, my mother's father and mother, were deported to Poland. Early on, I think in 1941. Mutti had a card from a neighbor in Düsseldorf. They'd arranged that before she left for England, in case anything happened to her parents. The card arrived from Switzerland; all it said was YOUR PARENTS HAVE RELOCATED TO LODZ. Jews from all over Germany were sent there. When the Russians liberated the camp in January, only a few hundred people were still alive."

"My father's Jewish and my mother's Aryan. I never knew my mother's parents. I met my grandfather, my father's father, only once. He said he was being sent to Poland too."

"I'm sure you'll have some news soon, Sophie. It's probably a great help to have one parent who's not Jewish, a protection."

How did the conversation turn so serious? I change the subject.

"What made you decide to be a nurse, Marianne? Is it fun living in the nurses' residence?"

"I always wanted to be a nurse. We do have fun, but the girls who join because they think uniforms are glamorous and they'll find a rich doctor to marry don't last long. Well, you know how hard the work is, Sophie. I don't know what's worse: never having enough hot water for a bath, or having to eat last night's supper when we come off night duty!

"Now, on that cheerful note, I'd better go or I'll be late for supper. See you on the ward on Saturday."

We hug each other good-bye.

· 13 ·

Aunt Em is waiting for me, wanting to hear all about Marianne. When I come to the part about Dr. O'Malley, she says, "What an extraordinary week. Dr. O'Malley suggested I get out of London for a few days. I've decided to go. It's the first holiday weekend since the war. It'll be quite an adventure. I might meet a mysterious person from the past too!"

"Aunt Em, you know everyone's always buried behind the newspaper. People only talk in air-raid shelters and thank goodness we don't need those anymore. Where will you go?"

"I thought I'd accept Uncle Gerald's invitation. It will give me the opportunity to settle dull business matters." She doesn't look at me.

Perhaps Aunt Em wants to discuss my adoption? After all, I have been sort of stranded with her for seven years.

"I'll take the 7:30 train on Friday morning. My friend Louisa lives fairly near, so I'll probably spend Saturday with her. That will ease the 'burden' for Winifred. Uncle Gerald will drive me back on Sunday night."

"Aunt Em, you surely won't leave a poor defenseless fourteen-year-old alone for the whole weekend? May Mandy come over, and would it be all right if she came early, to settle in before you leave?"

"I was going to ask Mrs. Gibson if you could go there."

"Please, Aunt Em, do let us stay here. We're not children anymore."

"I don't see why not. I'll walk over to Mrs. Gibson's now. It's a lovely evening. If Mandy's going to sleep in the spare room tomorrow, there's work to be done. You'll need to push all those Red Cross boxes I've been storing to the far wall. They'll have to be labeled too. The bed's made up, but the room should be aired and dusted."

I fling my arms around Aunt Em's neck. "Lovely, lovely Aunt Em."

"I recognize 'cupboard love,' Sophie Mandel. You don't fool me. Up you go then – get started."

Opening, labeling, and securing the boxes takes longer than I expect. There is one that must have got mixed in with the others by mistake. It is marked SOPHIE. I open it, thinking it might be outgrown clothes. Usually Aunt Em cuts them up for other things, or gives them to needy families. But the box only holds letters and drawings and a folder with my early report cards. I put it in my room to sort later.

* * *

Aunt Em comes in carrying a little vase of wildflowers from the garden. "Mrs. Gibson said Mandy could visit. So that's taken care of." She hands me a one pound note.

"That's an awful lot, Aunt Em. What's it for?"

"Call it a combination of emergency and fun money. I wouldn't want you to be destitute, without a penny in your pocket."

"Thank you very much, Aunt Em."

"Go to bed, dear. You've been having too many late nights. I'm surprised you haven't fallen asleep in class."

"It is a strain to keep awake sometimes, I admit."

Aunt Em laughs and kisses me good night. "I *am* pleased you found your friend again, Sophie."

On Thursday, when we go to pick up Mandy's things, Mrs. Gibson gives us homemade scones and Mandy's egg and bacon ration to take home for breakfast next day. Then we hear lecture number one about being responsible, and does Mandy have enough money, etc.

"Mother," Mandy says, "you'll see us Saturday, remember? I'm coming home right after my hospital shift to have tea with you before we go to the pictures. Sophie will pick me up when she's finished at nine o'clock so you can check us both over before we cycle home." She raises her left eyebrow at me.

Mandy loves the spare room. "Is this the wall next to your bed?"

"I think so."

We experiment for a while sending Morse code messages to each other. Over supper, we get lecture number two from Aunt Em about not coming in too late, and locking up and putting our bikes away, and then we have to write down a list of emergency numbers. We nod yes to everything, and stay up half the night gossiping.

On Friday morning, the taxi arrives for Aunt Em at 6:30. We wave her off and collapse in the kitchen.

"Alone at last," I say.

"Extra half hour in bed, or breakfast?" Mandy asks, yawning.

"I'll make us dried egg omelette, and we'll save the real eggs for tomorrow. You make the tea. The secret of making dried eggs slightly less revolting, Mandy, is to stir in the water very slowly so all the powder is dissolved. Not a lump in sight," I say, and pour the mixture into the hot pan. I grate a bit of cheese on top.

"Delicious," Mandy says, with her mouth full. "A bit like pancakes. Actually, I think keeping house is easy. I can't think why mothers make such a fuss about it."

It is fun coming home together to our "own" house. We have tea in the garden, and Mandy admits that Simon hopes to see her at the Youth Club tonight.

"He's so nice, Sophie. Let's go. It's mixed table tennis on Friday nights. Can I borrow your blue blouse?"

"Yes, and I want to borrow your black leather belt," I say.

"Done."

We get to the semifinals. Simon and Nigel are our partners and invite us to go to Fred's Fish Bar for chips. Later they walk us home.

"Night, Sophie. Don't get up in the morning. No point in us both losing our beauty sleep. See you after work tomorrow."

"Sleep well, Mandy."

I double-check the front door and the windows.

When I come down at nine next morning, there are two letters lying on the front mat. A bill for Aunt Em and a letter addressed to me c/o Miss Simmonds.

My letter is from someplace in Germany – not from Berlin, where my parents live. The return address on the back is marked U.S. ARMY HOSPITAL, MUNICH, GERMANY.

My mouth goes dry. This must be the letter I've been half expecting since the end of the war.

I can hear Mandy's voice in my head: "Why don't you open it, idiot?"

I can't. The minute I touch the envelope, I feel exactly the way I did on V-E night when I saw Marianne again.

Who else is going to appear from the past? Isn't that what Aunt Em said?

I sense the letter staring at me, urging me to open it.

The phone rings. It's Aunt Em.

"Oh, yes, everything's fine. No, there's nothing wrong. My

voice doesn't sound funny. It must be a bad connection. . . .
Tuesday . . . you're staying over for Whit Monday?"

*I'm repeating everything Aunt Em says. She must wonder what's
the matter with me.*

"Honestly, Aunt Em, I don't mind a bit. We're having fun. See
you Tuesday, then."

An envelope is a piece of paper, that's all. I draw two eyes and a
smiling mouth on the back. I slit open the envelope and pull out
a thin sheet of writing paper. It's dated May 21, 1945.

My Dearest Daughter,

Yes, I am alive. I have been in hospital since the U.S.
Army liberated Dachau Concentration Camp. An army
nurse is helping me write to you. I am making a good recov-
ery from typhus and feel a little stronger each day.

I hope this letter will reach you and that you and dear
Fräulein Margaret still live at the same address. I was so
worried that I would not remember it. Each night, before I
slept, I repeated the words and numbers.

I have sad news for you, Sophie. Your mother died on
January 12, 1943. The factory where she worked received a
direct hit in an air raid.

In February, in the last sweep to make Berlin *Judenrein* –
Jew free, I was picked up by the Gestapo. I was no longer a
"privileged" Jew, married to an Aryan.

Dear child, your mother and I spoke of you every day.
She was a loving and courageous woman.

83

I hope to leave the hospital before long and will look for work. There will have to be much rebuilding. I long to see you again. I pray it will be soon.

Write soon to your loving father,
Jacob Mandel

By the time I get to the end, I can't remember what I've read. My heart is pounding so hard, I can hear it thumping away. *Papa wants me back!*

I read the letter again slowly. Mama, Mama is dead.

It's my fault. I didn't wish hard enough for her to be safe.

· 14 ·

For a long time I sit reading and rereading every word. The signature at the bottom of the page looks as if the person who'd formed the letters is just learning to write. Jacob Mandel.

I don't know what I'm supposed to feel – should I be crying with joy that Papa's alive, or heartbroken that Mama's dead? It's hard being happy and sad at the same time. The feelings cancel each other out. It's as if I'm reading a letter meant for someone else. I can imagine telling Mandy, "Think how awful – she heard her mother died on the same day she found out that her father was still alive."

Last year I had to have a second tooth out. My left cheek was numb all day where the dentist froze it. That's how I feel inside, numb.

I read the letter once more, then fold it back along its original creases and replace it in the envelope. I put it in my pocket.

Mother died on January 12, 1943. That's two years and four months ago. *What was I doing that day? Why didn't I know? Shouldn't a person feel something when their mother dies? Have some kind of premonition at least?*

I always thought people got telegrams in one of those special buff-colored envelopes from the post office when someone dies. You couldn't send one, of course, not in the middle of the war, not from Germany.

I go into the sitting room and take Aunt Em's photograph album off the bookshelf. I turn the pages till I come to the "laughing girls."

If only you could speak to me. You're laughing, Mama. I can't remember the sound of your laugh. I wish I had more memories of you. Did you sing to me? Did you read me stories? What was your life really like? You should have explained to me why you sent me to be brought up by Aunt Em. Why did you say it was a holiday? Why didn't you tell me that we might never meet again?

I wish you'd known how happy I've been here. Would you under-stand and let me stay? Papa took that photo of you, when you were both so young, before you turned into my parents. One of you dead, the other a Jew from a concentration camp, ill with typhus.

At four fifteen, I leave for the hospital. All the way there I try to decide what to do if the worst happens: if Father wants me to go back to live with him in Germany and Aunt Em agrees because she thinks it's the "fair thing to do." If I run away, I could easily earn my living selling sketches and portraits. I could be a pavement artist. It wouldn't be any harder than painting white lines along curbs and lampposts in the blackout. I'd only agree to leave my garret and go back to school if Aunt Em promises to let me live with her forever. Yes, I know, it's blackmail. . . . It'd be worth it.

The porter greets me as if he's been waiting just for my arrival. "Don't look so glum, Miss. It's keeping so cheerful as keeps me going, as Mrs. Mop says." I manage a smile. Our porter's a Tommy Handley fan, always quoting from everyone's favorite radio show: "It's that man again – ITMA." Aunt Em and I try never to miss a program.

"Thank goodness for an extra pair of hands." Staff Nurse rattles off instructions as if afraid an emergency might arrive in the ward before she's finished telling me what to do.

After I've made up the beds, and my "hospital corners" won a smile of approval from Staff Nurse, I mop the bathroom, arrange all the screens for visitors, and am sent down to the kitchen to remind them about sending up the special trays for the diabetics. Then I refill the water jugs and am in the middle of dusting the radiators, when I am told I can go for a ten minute break.

Marianne passes me on the stairs. "Can't stop, Sophie, I'm being moved to 'maternity.' Bridget's home. I'll call you soon. The three of us must meet." She squeezes my arm.

At nine o'clock, when my shift ends, I'm just thankful I've made it through. My legs feel as if they've run a five minute mile. I think I forgot to eat today.

* * *

At the Gibsons' house, Nigel opens the door. "Hello, Sophie. Mother and Mandy aren't home from the pictures yet. What's new?"

"My mother's dead."

He stares, horrified. "I'm sorry, Sophie." He puts his arms round me and pats my back as though I'm a baby.

I want to go on standing there in the half-light of the hallway, to put my head on his shoulder and cry. Of course, I don't. "I had a letter from my father."

"When?"

The front door opens. Nigel and I turn away from each other.

"Hello, sorry we're late. You should have come, Nigel. Mum was petrified."

"Don't exaggerate, Mandy. Now, shall we all have some cocoa before you girls cycle home?"

"Please. Any biscuits, Mother?" Mandy follows her into the kitchen.

"Nigel, don't tell them yet. I'll tell Mandy myself."

"All right."

"Come on, you two, stop whispering. I thought I was going to scream when Charles Boyer was creeping around the attic looking for Ingrid Bergman's jewelry. I shan't sleep a wink tonight." Mandy chatters on and on, so I don't need to talk much.

"Thanks awfully for the cocoa, Mrs. Gibson," I say.

"Nigel, it's late. Cycle home with the girls, please. You look so tired, Sophie. Is there anything wrong?"

"It was a bit frantic on the ward tonight, Mrs. Gibson."

"Come on, twin, let's be on our way." Nigel hurries Mandy out.

The moment Nigel leaves us and I close the front door, Mandy bursts out: "What's going on? All of a sudden I'm shut out. First it's your friend Marianne and now Nigel."

"Mandy, what are you talking about?"

"Don't pretend, Sophie. I could tell as soon as Mum and I came into the house. Do you think I'm blind and deaf? Since when do we keep secrets from each other?"

I hang up my blazer and walk into the kitchen. I need to sit down.

"Don't walk away from me when I'm talking to you, Sophie Mandel!"

"I'm not. Stop bullying me, Mandy."

"Did something happen to upset you? Was there a death on the ward?"

"Not on the ward. Somewhere else." I pull the letter out of my pocket and push it over to her. "Read it. I'm going to bed. Good night."

I brush my teeth, get into pajamas, and sit on my bed and hold Monkey.

Mandy knocks on the door and comes in before I have a chance to answer. She throws herself at me. "Sophie, dearest Soph, I'm a selfish jealous pig. I'm so very sorry. Why didn't you tell me? Please please forgive me." She gives me the letter back.

I almost laugh. She's so tragic. "Don't be humble, Mandy, you didn't know. The letter only came after you left this morning. I told Nigel because he was the one to open the door. If you'd opened it, I would have told you first. . . . You know what upsets me, Mandy? Not just that she's been dead for so long without my knowing, though that's bad enough, but the awful waste. She had me and sent me away before I was old enough to really know her. She cut herself off from her family, well they both did, so I never knew my relatives."

"She saved your father, didn't she? You're alive. That's two lives. How can you call that a waste?"

I don't answer. I can't think logically.

Mandy tiptoes out as if I'm ill.

One part of me is mourning and the other part is terrified of losing the person who became my "foster mother" all these years. My brain's going in a million directions.

I'm fourteen years old – I think I have the right to decide about my life. . . . I'll write to the Home Office. They decide about naturalization, visas, passports, and things like that. How do I convince the Minister I'm the right "material" to become a loyal British subject? What I need is a letter of reference from someone in a position of authority – a person who is willing to say I'm doing a job of national importance and deserve British citizenship. Once I've got that, no one can send me anywhere I don't want to go.

There's the headmistress, but I hardly think helping in the library would be considered crucial. It's got to be an essential service, like coal mining or driving an ambulance. . . . Why didn't I think of that before? *The hospital.* I'll ask Matron. She's very imposing. Everyone's in awe of her. The nurses say she's aware of everything that goes on anywhere in the building. The Middlesex has a terrific reputation.

I even spoke to Matron once. She was walking down the corridor, with a chart in her hand, doctors in tow. I flattened myself against the wall and said, "Good morning, Madam," and she sort of nodded in my direction. A letter from her saying I'm indispensable would be nearly as good as a recommendation from the king.

It is almost four in the morning before I'm satisfied with my efforts:

Dear Matron,

I am one of the Junior Red Cross cadets in your hospital. At present I work a Saturday afternoon and evening shift. I look forward to being there each week and hope that, in a small way, I can help to make the hospital run even more smoothly than it does already. *A bit of flattery never hurts.* I am in the process of applying for British citizenship and would greatly appreciate a note from you supporting my application.

It is vital for me to be allowed to remain in this country and not be returned to Germany, my place of birth. After seven years in England, my complete loyalty is to the country that has given me refuge.

Thank you very much for your time and consideration,

Yours truly,

Sophie Mandel

Then I draw a cartoon of a cadet making beds, taking temperatures, and scrubbing bedpans, and a nurse looking on, smiling approvingly. I add a balloon shape with the words: "How could we ever manage without you?"

· 15 ·

After Mandy leaves, I cycle to the hospital to ask the porter to deliver my letter to Matron personally. That way she'll get it almost immediately. He says he'll take it on his tea break.

The house seems eerily quiet when I get back. You can tell there's been a death. Even though it happened in a foreign country two years ago, somehow the news of it lingers in the air.

Poor Mama, not even to have a funeral. I know that happens a lot in wartime, but when it's my own mother who is buried under piles of rubble, it's so horrible I want to scream; do anything to stop thinking about her like that.

I close my eyes, trying to remember something about her when she was alive. She used to hum when she worked. Even when she was sewing, she'd hum through a mouthful of pins. Once I asked her, "What's the song about, Mama?" She'd said, "I don't know all the words, but once upon a time there was a boy and he saw a little rose standing in the meadow."

Sah ein Knab' ein Röslein Steh'n
Röslein auf der Heiden . . .

Until this moment, I'd totally forgotten that. *Was the rose a flower or a girl?* It doesn't matter.

It's going to rain, the sun's gone in. My window's wide-open. I rush upstairs to shut it. While I'm making my bed, I stub my toe on the box marked SOPHIE. I drag it out and undo the lid. It looks as if Aunt Em has kept most of my early report cards: "Sophie is settling down well." "Her drawing shows promise." "Sophie's spelling needs attention."

The usual. Everything neatly tied up in a cardboard folder, a thick gray one. A rubber band to keep the contents in place. There's a copy of my school registration form. All it says is the day I started school – January 9, 1939. Aunt Em must have kept me home those first few weeks in England, to give me a chance to learn some English, I expect. In the box where it says NAME OF PARENT OR GUARDIAN, there's Aunt Em's name. That should help my chances with the Home Office – having a solid British citizen as my guardian all these years.

There are some of my early drawings too. One is of a gruesome-looking old woman glaring at two little girls. Underneath I'd printed: PLEAS CAN WE CUM HOME? That must have been when I was still an evacuee.

There are two letters in German, one dated 3 *Januar* 1939, and the other one a month later – 1 *Februar* 1939. Those are the only words I can still read, other than the greeting and the signature and a row of O's instead of X's, the way we write them over here.

I remember how angry the letters made me feel then. There was the day Aunt Em handed me the envelope and I'd torn off the stamp for Nigel's stamp collection. I'd burst out rudely: "I don't know how to read this letter and I don't want to. It's too hard. We don't write like that in school."

Aunt Em must have written to my parents and explained because there's one more letter addressed to me in the file. This time it's printed in English, and says:

Dear Sophie,

Thank you for your letter. You write very good English. Papa and I are well. Today I went for a walk in the Grunewald, our green forest. I waved to Papa, and watched him cut a hedge into the shape of a little bird. He says he would like to be a bird and fly to England to visit you.

Love from your mama and papa OOOOO

There's a drawing of a bird-shaped hedge at the bottom of the page. The date on the letter is August 15, 1939, two weeks before the outbreak of World War Two. That day Aunt Em explained to me that we'd have to wait until the end of the war before there would be any more letters from my parents.

Another letter, addressed to Aunt Em, is from a Quaker group in Berlin. It's postmarked November 14, 1938 – that's when I still lived in Berlin. Aunt Em had clipped a column from a January 2, 1939 *Times* to the envelope. She'd circled NEW ANTI-JEWISH MEASURES IN GERMANY, and then a quote from a Quaker group: JEWS DESPERATE TO LEAVE.

Snooping's horrible. But if this is something really private, why would Aunt Em leave it in a box marked SOPHIE? I have to read it.

November 14, 1938
Berlin

Dear Margaret,

I think our days are numbered here. I don't know how much longer the Nazi government will tolerate our presence. I'm sure they'll close down the office.

The world reports on the "action" taken against the Jewish people on November 9 and 10 are not exaggerated. In fact, they cannot accurately describe the viciousness of the attacks against men, women, and children, under the benign eye of officialdom. Burning, looting, and imprisonment of Jews. We are able to help so few to get out of Germany. Desperate men and women, some with babies in arms, sit helplessly in the corridors waiting to be placed on some kind of list that will get them to safety.

I'll talk more to you in the new year, when I hope to be back at home.

Affectionately and in haste,
Louisa

Mama wasn't in that kind of danger – she wasn't Jewish. I wonder if she guessed what it might be like marrying Papa. She was very brave to stand by him.

Tucked down inside the flap of the cardboard is a luggage label on a string. I remember wearing that on the *Kindertransport*. We all wore them. My number was two hundred and seventeen. What's that bit of old blanket doing in there . . .? *Käthe?*

Sophie Mandel, you're too old to cry over a doll. . . .

We're going to have a party. Mama, Papa, and me. It's my birth-day. I run all the way home from school and Mama is waiting at the door.

She ties a scarf round my eyes. Papa's voice asks: "How many fingers can you see?"

I shout: "None." In the living room, I tear off the blindfold. Papa throws me in the air seven times, *himmelhoch* – sky-high, because I'm seven today.

The cake is on the table; it is chocolate and white, in the shape of a ring. Mama has sprinkled powdered sugar over the top. It looks like snow crystals. I have a present too – a box tied with blue ribbon. I lift the lid. It is the doll from the window of the big toy shop near Mama's work. She has light brown hair. It is parted in the middle. Her hair is braided. She wears a skirt and a pullover. There are real white socks and leather shoes on her feet.

"What will you call her?" Papa asks me.

"Her name is Käthe," I answer, and hug her to my chest.

Next day is Saturday, and we go for a picnic in the woods. Papa knows the names of all the trees. I do too. Pine and spruce and beech.

Mama pours coffee from a thermos. There's milk for me. We sit on the blanket and finish the birthday cake. Then we play hide-and-seek. It is Papa's turn to hide. I count to a hundred, hiding my eyes on Mama's lap. When I open them, there are two shadows on the blanket, tall like trees. They are not trees. They are men wearing black boots and uniforms with silver buttons. They smile at Mama. "*Ganz allein, Gnädige Frau* – All alone, dear lady?" I move closer to Mama. She holds my hand so tight she squishes my fingers. I want to go and find Papa. He will think I've forgotten him. *Poor Papa*, waiting to be found.

"It is the little one's birthday. Tell the gentlemen how old you are, Liebchen." I pull my hand away from Mama's and hold up seven fingers.

"Three cups and plates, and who else is in this party?" They stare at Mama – they are not smiling now.

"It is Käthe, my new doll." I hold her up – close to me, so they can't touch her.

"Happy birthday. *Heil Hitler*." The boots click and move away. When they are gone, I help Mama fold the blanket.

Papa comes over to us from behind the tree, where he was hiding. We go home. When I put Käthe to bed, I tell her not to be frightened of the soldiers. "I will always take care of you, my little Käthe."

. 16 .

For years I've been afraid to look at Käthe. It was all right at first, when that nice girl, whose name I've forgotten, twisted Käthe's head back after the Gestapo left the train. It was all right when Marianne was with me, but after that I was afraid to look at Käthe, convinced there'd be a jagged scar where the officer's hands had touched her neck – that somehow it had grown there.

Käthe, my Käthe. You look perfect. There isn't a mark on you.

I hold the doll for a while and then wrap the blanket snugly round her and put her back in her box bed.

That's how I'll think of you, Mama – perfect, without a blemish. I won't think about the damage bombs and broken glass can do. I'll remember you rolling out pastry, or letting me come to the shop to help you, or hugging Papa when he came home from work or upset because you were worried the Nazis might hurt him.

When I give Käthe to my daughter, I'll tell her it was you who sewed the dress. I'll say, "This is a present from your grandmother, the one who lived in Germany long ago."

I go downstairs and settle down to write to my father. Someone's at the back door. *Mandy?* She'll wonder why Aunt Em isn't here. It's stupid of me not to have told her the truth. I could have said I need time to be alone for a bit.

"Nigel, I wasn't expecting you. I mean, come in."

"Thanks, I can only stay a minute. Swotting for my science exam. Mother sent me over with a loaf for your tea. She's been baking. Is your aunt back yet?"

"Not yet. Thanks, awfully. I was just going to write to my father. Hard to know what to say."

"Rotten luck to hear like that, but it's great news about your dad."

"Somehow I'd never thought about one of my parents dying. To be honest, I didn't think very much about them at all. Do you think I'll be allowed to choose who I live with? *There, I've finally said it out aloud – the thing I'm most afraid of. If I can't go on living with Aunt Em, it means I'll lose friends, country, everything I know. How many times in a lifetime am I supposed to do that?* Got time for a cup of tea?" I put the kettle on.

Nigel perches on the corner of the kitchen table. "You know how we always had these huge family gatherings at Christmas? On Boxing Day, the last one before the war, Uncle Bert asked me in front of everyone: 'Tell me, son, who's your favorite – your mum or your dad?' There'd been lots of talking and laughing, and suddenly all those hot red faces looked at me, waiting for an answer. Asking me to choose. Whatever I'd say, I'd hurt someone's feelings. I was afraid I was going to cry. Mandy saved me. She jumped on Dad's lap and said, 'Well, I love my daddy to bits.' They all laughed and I ran upstairs and wouldn't come down again.

"Dad came to my room later and brought me a slice of Christmas cake and the last cracker. I gave it to Mandy. It had a thimble and a paper crown in it. People think kids don't matter, that they don't have feelings. It'll be all right, Soph. I'll see you soon, science calls."

I return to my letter.

16, Great Tichfield Street
London WC1
May 23, 1945

Dear Father:

I am glad you are feeling stronger. The nurses seem to be taking good care of you. It was a shock to hear about Mother. I'm sorry.

Aunt Em told me about the holiday she had in Germany when she first met you. We have a photograph of Mother that you took the day before you got engaged. It's beautiful. I'm sorry, so sorry, that things didn't turn out the way they were supposed to.

This is a holiday weekend. Aunt Em is visiting her brother in the country. I will tell her when she comes back. She will be glad about you and sad about Mama, as of course am I.

I'm fourteen now. Aunt Em thinks I look a bit like both of you. Get well soon.

> Your affectionate daughter,
>
> Sophie Mandel

After I finish the letter, I get out my sketchbook and begin a family portrait. First I draw Grandpa Mandel, with his silver and white prayer shawl, the fringes hanging below his waist. *Papa must have told me it's a prayer shawl.* I draw his face in shadow, the way it looked that time in the synagogue. I draw candles flickering round the walls. Papa, his hand on my shoulder, and myself as a little girl, looking up at him. I sketch Mama in her best dress, the one with the big lace collar, and her hair in wispy curls round her forehead. I have no idea what Mama's parents looked like. She never mentioned her father.

When I was small, I wondered what happened to the baby in the cradle in the photo of the Mandels, the photo that Papa had to hide from the Nazis. He told me once, "That's my baby sister in the crib. My mother – your grandmother – died when the baby was only a few months old." I expect my aunt kept house for Grandpa Mandel when she grew up.

I draw Aunt Em on the next page, with her kind eyes and the little wrinkles round them. She's never tried to take Mother's place, but she's the most perfect aunt anyone could ask for.

· 17 ·

On Tuesday morning I arrive at school just as orchestra practice ends. Mandy must have spread the word because Sally Jones, who I usually try to avoid, simpers up to me and says, "Sorry to hear about your mother. When are you going back to live in Germany with your father?"

I mumble something noncommittal.

Is the whole world waiting for me to be sent back there?

I sit down on the bench in the cloakroom. For a minute I can't think where I'm supposed to be heading.

"Sophie, come on, we'll be late for prayers." Mandy pulls me to my feet and drags me down the corridor to Assembly.

"What did Aunt Em say?"

"Nothing."

"Well, what did you tell her?"

"I haven't."

"Why haven't you?"

"If you must know, because she's not coming home till this afternoon."

We sit.

"You mean, you stayed by yourself for two whole nights?" Mandy hisses in my ear.

"Yes."

"Weren't you frightened?"

"Of what? Charles Boyer looking for my jewelry?"

We stand in silence as the staff file in and take their places on the platform.

Later, as we go into class, I remember I'd left my history notes in the cloakroom.

"Hurry up, we'll be late. You know how Miss Jasper hates that," Mandy says.

"I didn't ask you to wait, and please stop telling me what to do."

I walk away from her. Miss Jasper doesn't hear me enter the class. She's writing on the blackboard. I copy the question into my notebook: HOW DID THE INDUSTRIAL REVOLUTION AFFECT THE WORKING CLASSES IN THE NINETEENTH CENTURY? *Words. They don't mean anything to me.*

When the bell rings at the end of the first period, Mandy sweeps past me, talking to Sally. Instead of going to English, I walk into the cloakroom, fetch my hat, and saunter out of school.

I wish I'd stayed home. Joanne Fisher did when her brother's ship was torpedoed, with all hands lost at sea. Anthea Warren was away a whole week when her father died in a Japanese prisoner of war camp.

Aunt Em will be home soon. What am I going to tell her? How shall I do it?

The moment I get back, I dial the nurses' residence. I badly want to talk to Marianne. A soft Scot's burr informs me that Nurse Kohn left that morning on a leave of absence.

Voices in the hall.

"Aunt Em, you're early. I'm so glad you're back. Hello, Uncle Gerald, Aunt Winifred."

Aunt Em hugs me, obviously pleased to be home – worn-out with listening to Aunt Winifred, I should think. "Sophie, everything looks beautifully tidy. Did you and Mandy have a nice time?"

Aunt Winifred interrupts before I have a chance to reply. "You must be getting quite excited about going home, Sophie."

What on earth is she talking about?

"Going home, Aunt Winifred? I *am* home."

Aunt Em sits down. Uncle Gerald takes his pipe from his breast pocket, turns to me and says, "Would you find me a match, my dear? I must have left mine in the car."

I hand him the box on the mantelpiece above the fireplace. *Surely he can see it there?*

"No, dear, I mean your real home – in Germany with your parents. I expect all you children will be on your way soon. Isn't that so, Gerald?"

I look at Aunt Winifred's carefully marcelled hair, the silly little hat she wears, her slightly caked bright lipstick.

I hate her! I really truly hate her and I think I'm going to tell her so.

"Why are you staring at me in that way, child?"

"Because it's none of your business."

Aunt Em's shocked "Sophie, apologize to Aunt Winifred at once" is exactly what I don't need to hear at this moment.

"I will not and she's not my aunt any more than you are."

I manage to get myself out of the room without crying or slamming the door. I hear Uncle Gerald saying, "Must be getting along, Margaret," as I go upstairs, then Aunt Em's response, which I can't hear, and their footsteps going into the kitchen. I suppose they'll all have a "nice" cup of tea while they discuss how fast they can get rid of me.

And I haven't even had a chance to tell Aunt Em about Mama.

It's ages before the front door opens and closes. Moments later, Aunt Em calls me to come downstairs. She's putting away the tea things. "Would you mind telling me exactly what that exhibition was about?"

"Mine, or Aunt Winifred's?" I feel the teapot; it's still warm. I pour myself a cup of tea.

"I want an explanation, and you will give it to me in a civilized manner."

"Perhaps you'd better read this first." I hand Aunt Em Papa's letter, and turn away to drink my tea. When I hear her blow her nose, I wait a few minutes before turning round. She is almost composed again.

"Sophie, my dear. Why didn't you tell me? I would have come home at once." Her hands, holding the letter, tremble a little. She puts the page on the table between us and clasps her fingers together tightly.

"You've got so tall, Sophie. I wish Charlotte. . . . Jacob won't recognize you."

"Aunt Em, please *please* don't send me back to Germany. I'm afraid to live there. I won't know anyone. I can't speak the language. Of course I love my father, but I hardly remember him and he doesn't know anything about me. I thought I belonged here with you."

"Sophie, Aunt Winifred's words were out of place and premature. No one is going to send you anywhere immediately."

"Never – I won't go."

"Listen to me. Don't interrupt, please. I always knew I only had you on loan until it was safe for you to rejoin your parents. I thought you understood that. Didn't I make it clear to you?"

"No. You didn't, Aunt Em. All you ever said was, after the war there'd be letters. Every time I wanted to talk about what was going to happen then, you changed the subject. I'm not a thing to be shuffled back and forth. Doesn't what *I* want matter at all? Don't you want me to stay?"

"What you or I want isn't the point, Sophie. You have a father who loves you and who has lost everything except you. Your parents trusted me and I will never break that trust."

I'm fighting for my life.

"It's not fair," I blurt out.

Aunt Em doesn't reply.

Oh, Aunt Em, why can't you try to keep me with you? Why can't you admit that I'm the daughter you didn't have? It's hopeless. You never will. I understand. You can't. I'll just have to go on with my plans without your help.

"Sophie, your mother was my dear friend. I shall miss her very much. I know how hard losing her must be for you. Remember, you have a father who longs to see you and get to know you again. This is what is important. Now let's make plans. It will take time to get a visitor's permit for your father, but I'm sure, in view of the circumstances, the Home Office will cooperate. He won't have recovered sufficiently from his illness to travel yet, but I'll start setting things in motion tomorrow.

"Time for me to unpack. Later on we might start on a list of things to send to Jacob in hospital."

End of discussion. As usual.

"Aunt Em, I wrote to Father earlier. I'll go and post the letter now, if you don't mind."

"Do. I'll speak to Uncle Gerald and Aunt Winifred later. Under the circumstances, I shall apologize on your behalf."

"Thanks, Aunt Em." I hug her.

"Sophie, you do understand, don't you?"

I pour away the tea – it's stone-cold now. I run the tap so I don't have to answer.

After I post my letter, I wait outside Mandy's gate till she comes home from school. She walks straight past me as if I'm invisible.

"Mandy, I've got something to say to you."

"Again? I thought you'd finished."

"I'm sorry. I was awfully rude and I didn't mean it."

"Yes, you did. You're right. I am bossy. Mum's always telling me."

"I had a fight with Aunt Winifred."

"Metaphorically, I hope."

"It nearly wasn't and then I started on Aunt Em."

"Do you want to come in and tell me all the gory details?"

"I will, but not today. Aunt Em's a bit upset. I'd better get home."

"My *Girl's Crystal* just came – you can read it first." Mandy hands me her magazine.

"Thanks, awfully."

"I've come to the conclusion that Sally is a stuck-up, big-mouthed snob."

When I get back, Aunt Em says, "I phoned the headmistress. She agrees with me that you should stay home this week, but she wants you to continue revising for the June exams."

"Does she know I walked out of school?"

"It was not discussed, so I think you may forget about it."

· 18 ·

On Wednesday, when Aunt Em comes home from the office, she says, "I've been making some enquiries through the Red Cross. Things in Europe are pretty chaotic. I'm told, much worse than the London Blitz. Thousands and thousands of homeless people, soldiers returning from war, cities reduced to rubble, and hardly any food. If the war had lasted any longer, many people would have died of starvation. I know you'll keep this confidential, Sophie, but it's almost certain that our own rations will be cut again in the next few months. Rationing may go on for years."

"I always thought the moment war was over, food would miraculously reappear in the shops. I've begun making a list for Father's parcel, Aunt Em. Shall I read it to you? I tried to think what the patients in our hospital seem to want most: instant coffee, tea, biscuits, condensed milk, tinned fruit, soap, socks. I've still got that bar of Yardley's soap Aunt Winifred gave me for Christmas – we could send that."

"Add cigarettes. Even if your father doesn't smoke, cigarettes can be exchanged for almost anything. I hadn't thought of socks, but I can knit a pair quite quickly. There's some of that gray wool left from your last winter's cardigan. Shirts. We must assume that Jacob has no clothes except what the hospital may provide."

"There's a whole boxful of men's shirts in the boxes I labeled last week."

"Why don't you see if you can find one or two shirts in a plain color, dear? Your father is exactly the kind of recipient those shirts are meant for."

I rush upstairs. I know why Aunt Em said shirts in a plain color. We've both seen too many pictures of prisoners in striped jackets lately. I find a blue one and a white one, both in good condition.

"I tried some on, Aunt Em. These reach to my knees and the sleeves are miles too long, so they should be all right. I expect Father's pretty thin."

"Excellent. Bring the shopping basket, Sophie, and we'll see what we can do."

On our way to the grocer's, we pass Mr. Billy's. There's a notice in the window: NO LAMB, BEEF, OR OFFAL. Mr. Billy is standing in the shop doorway.

"Good day, Miss Simmonds. Haven't seen you in a while." He leers at me.

Aunt Em nods politely. "Good afternoon, Mr. Billy. I wonder if you might have any tins of meat today? We're putting together a care package for a friend in Europe. People are having a bad time over there."

"Tins of meat, Miss Simmonds? That's a joke. Haven't you heard? There's a peace on. If I did come across such a thing, and I say *if* . . . well, charity begins at home, Madam. Meat for the enemy – that's a good one. Good day, Madam, Miss."

"I think, Sophie," Aunt Em says, "we must try to find another butcher to register with. I really don't want to have any more dealings with Mr. Billy. In future we shall shop elsewhere."

"What did you expect, Aunt Em?"

"Decency. He really is a most odious man."

We walk in silence to the grocer's.

I give our list to Mrs. Logan, and she looks at us as if we've gone mad. Her eyebrows shoot up to her hair net. Aunt Em puts our ration books on the counter.

"No need to look so astonished, Mrs. Logan. We're putting together a parcel for a friend in hospital, in Germany. He's recovering from typhus. Is this list too unrealistic?"

I realize suddenly that Aunt Em intentionally does not mention who the parcel is for. I hope she doesn't think I'd be embarrassed.

"It's for my father, actually," I say.

"In that case, we'll have to see what we can do, won't we?"

Mrs. Logan reappears five minutes later. "Digestive biscuits – you don't want anything too rich. I can let you have some Bovril cubes too – very strengthening. There's a tin of peaches. I'm sorry about the sugar, but you can have a tin of golden syrup."

"We're truly grateful, Mrs. Logan."

"We must all be that, Miss Simmonds. This time let's hope the peace lasts."

After she takes our points, she puts a tin of corned beef in the basket. "No charge. That's from me to your father, Sophie. My dad didn't come back from the war in 1918. You send that with my good wishes. That'll be nineteen shillings and eight pence, please."

I put a pound note – the one that Aunt Em had given me to spend – on the counter.

"Thank you, Mrs. Logan. It's very kind of you."

When we get back from our shopping expedition, the afternoon post has arrived. There is a letter for me from Middlesex Hospital.

May 24, 1945

Dear Miss Mandel,

I am pleased to hear that you find your time with us so rewarding. The dedicated work of Junior Red Cross cadets is invaluable in nursing homes and hospitals across the British Isles.

With your permission, I will ask Sister Tutor to include your drawing in our next staff newsletter. Wishing you every success.

Yours truly and on behalf of Matron,
L.A. Ransome

I enclose the letter with my application to the Home Office, and send it off next morning.

On Friday Mandy and Nigel call on their way to the Youth Club, and ask if I want them to put my name forward for next year's planning committee. I tell them to go ahead.

I'll be here. Matron's letter will work, I know it will.

Aunt Em's rule is that if I don't go to school, I can't go out socially either. She does agree to let me do my hospital shift as usual on Saturday.

Marianne telephones from the nurses' residence just before I leave for work.

"I'm back, Sophie. I don't go on the ward till Monday. Bridget wants to meet you. Are you free Sunday? I could call for you around two and we can go for a walk first."

"Who is it?" Aunt Em comes into the hall.

"Marianne. She's invited me to tea on Sunday. Is it all right if I go?"

"It'll do you good."

Marianne arrives early. The first thing she says to me is, "You're looking awfully tired, Sophie. Are you getting enough sleep?"

"We had some bad news – at least . . ."

I still haven't worked out how to say it's both good and bad.

"Let's go and sit in Regent's Park – we've got time," she says.

We sit watching the swans swimming in elegant circles, ignoring the chattering ducks.

· 19 ·

"While you were away, Marianne . . . ," I begin.
"Do you know why I had to go home?" She starts speaking at the same time. "You first, Sophie. Is it something to do with Aunt Em?"

"In a way it is because she and my mother were friends. A letter arrived from my father –"

"Then he's safe . . . ," Marianne interrupts. "That's wonderful news."

"Yes. He's recuperating from typhus in a hospital in Munich."

"I thought you said your parents lived in Berlin?"

"My mother died there in an air raid. The factory where she worked got a direct hit. That was in 1943. My father wrote he was picked up and sent to a camp called Dachau. The Americans liberated him three weeks ago."

Marianne takes my hand. "Sorry is such a little word. People use it all the time, don't they? When they make a mistake, or drop something, or bump into you in the blackout. I wish I knew how to . . ." She seems to be having trouble keeping her voice steady.

"Marianne, do you think Mama knew she wouldn't see me again? Is that why she didn't make any promises, or say I'll see you in a little while, or when your holiday's over? I mean, she just handed me over, like a puppy you can't keep any longer."

"I think my father had a feeling that he wouldn't see us again too." Marianne's voice is low.

When I look at her, tears are rolling down her cheeks. After a few minutes, she wipes her face with the back of her hand. By this time I'm crying too.

"Mother heard from the Red Cross," Marianne says. "That's why I got leave. In 1942, Father was sent to Terezin, a concentration camp near Prague. It was liberated by the Russians on V-E Day. The letter said he died of malnutrition – a kind way of saying of hunger – at the end of April."

Marianne turns to me. She'd kept her head averted till then, as if she couldn't finish what she had to say if she looked at me. "It's not fair. Another week and the war would have been over. He'd never hurt anyone. He loved his books and he loved us. Hunted down and starved to death. . . ."

"Because he was a Jew." I finish the sentence for her.

I touch my neck, feeling the choking sensation I felt the first time I'd tried on my Star of David that I keep hidden away in a cubbyhole in my desk. *Had Mama been trying to save me from being*

*punished, the way she'd been for marrying a Jew? From suffering like
my father, or being starved to death like Mr. Kohn?*

People pass by on their Sunday outings. No one takes any
notice of us.

"I hope you'll see your father soon, Sophie."

I was going to tell Marianne how hard I was trying not to
leave England and go and live with Papa in Germany. *How can I
tell her now?*

"Aunt Em's hoping to bring him over for a visit."

"I'm glad." Marianne opens her handbag, takes out a powder
compact, and dabs at her cheeks. "Look at me, Sophie. Awful.
You're supposed to make a good impression on Bridget and her
parents." She pats my face with the powder puff.

"You're always telling me to make a good impression." I sneeze.
Actually I enjoy her "big sister" act.

"Gesundheit."

"I think I'll have to disgrace you with my shiny nose." I sneeze
again. "Anything with perfume always makes me sneeze."

"You're hopeless." She smiles at me. "Come on, or we'll be
late."

We run for the bus.

At Circus Road, Marianne points out Bridget's house, "That big
one on the corner of St. Anne's Terrace. Number twenty-two."

"Mary Anne. It *is* Mary Anne, isn't it?" A thin-lipped woman
wearing a black straw hat comes toward us.

"Good afternoon, Mrs. Abercrombie Jones."

"What a surprise to see you after all these years. And is this your sister?"

"No, this is my friend, Sophie Mandel. You'll have to excuse us – we're on our way to visit Bridget O'Malley."

"You kept in touch, did you? My husband will be so interested to hear I've met you again. You've quite grown up."

"Is Gladys still with you?"

"She left. Joined the forces. It's impossible to find good help these days. Are your parents well?"

"Actually, my father died recently in a concentration camp in Czechoslovakia. Do you remember once you said to me that he must wait his turn like other refugees? 'It is not a question of saving, but of good manners.'"

"My dear Mary Anne, we had no possible way of knowing."

"I suppose not. Good-bye, Mrs. Abercrombie Jones."

Marianne links her arm through mine. "That felt good. I used to call her Aunt Wera, instead of Vera, before I could speak English properly. It used to drive her mad."

A slim girl with short dark curly hair runs down the steps to greet us. She kisses Marianne on both cheeks, then shakes hands with me.

"I'm so pleased to see you both. Do come in. We're going to have tea in the garden."

"How nice to see you again, Sophie." Dr. O'Malley emerges from his study to greet us. His arms go round Marianne and he murmurs: "My dear child, we are all deeply grieved for you and your mother. We have written to her."

Bridget and Marianne begin to cry, and then Mrs. O'Malley hugs us both and says, "Come along with me now. Dry your eyes and let's have tea." She plies us with bread and honey that her sister sent from Galway in Ireland, chocolate biscuits Bridget brought back from Canada, and homemade Irish soda bread.

Bridget is what Aunt Em would call a character. She talks nonstop, about Canada.

"I've learned to curl and ski and skate and speak French, but there's nowhere like home." She kisses her mother's cheek, and I think, *I'll never be able to do that.*

The three of us do the dishes and then go upstairs to Bridget's room.

"Presents." Bridget tosses a beautifully wrapped parcel into Marianne's arms.

"Bridget!" Marianne shrieks.

Bridget says quickly, "Don't you dare say you'll never wear them."

"Thank you a million times. I've never in my whole life owned a pair of nylon stockings."

"Well, now you've got two pairs. They won't ladder if you roll them on very carefully – I'll show you how."

"I'm not going to wear them. I'll just look at them."

"I knew it was a waste to give them to you. I'll just have to take them back, I suppose."

"I *will* wear them. But it will have to be a very special occasion. Thank you, dear Bridget."

"This is for you, Sophie. I'm afraid it's only a small box of chocolates. I didn't know we were going to meet, you see."

"It's very kind of you, Bridget. Thank you."

I undo the blue ribbon, the tissue paper, and the little gold seal and offer the chocolates around.

"Heaven! It melts in your mouth," Marianne mumbles. "Six months of chocolate rations in there, Sophie."

Bridget refuses to take one. "I've been spoiled long enough. These are for you, Sophie. Now if you two can stop eating for a minute, I'm ready for a proper talk."

"Isn't that what we've been having?" I ask innocently.

Marianne and Bridget look at each other.

"All right, Bridget, confession time. Is it fit for Sophie to hear?"

"Of course it is. I've been bursting to tell you. I've met someone."

"You've only been home a few days," Marianne says.

"Don't interrupt, I'm going to tell you everything. On Tuesday, I had my appointment with Matron. I can't tell you how nervous I was, but she was perfectly charming. Glanced at my Canadian hospital records and said, 'It all seems very satisfactory.' I'm to begin on Monday week. I was so relieved that I ran down the front steps of the hospital, and went flying."

"Into the arms of a handsome stranger?" Marianne says.

"Almost. Everything in my purse scattered all over the sidewalk."

"It's hard to believe, Bridget O'Malley, that you once lectured me on speaking English. What is your 'purse' and could you please translate 'sidewalk' for us poor English girls?"

"A purse is a handbag and the sidewalk is the pavement. Now for the exciting part. A young man in an air force uniform helped me up and asked me if I was hurt. The Royal Canadian Air Force, can you imagine? By the time we'd gathered my things, we'd introduced ourselves. His name is Dominic St. Pierre. He's from Longueuil, which is on the outskirts of Montreal. He's twenty-two, and he wants me to go out with him again."

"Again? Bridget O'Malley, I'm shocked. He's a perfect stranger."

I know Marianne is only pretending to be horrified.

"We went to have a cup of coffee in Fullers. He asked for my phone number, and whether he could take me out. Marianne, don't look so scandalized! He's a most respectable Canadian boy, I can tell. I'll ask him to come to the house first to meet Mother."

"Just so long as you don't fall in love with him and go and live in Canada and leave us again," Marianne says.

When it is time to go home, Dr. O'Malley insists on driving us both.

Mrs. O'Malley says, "I hope Marianne will bring you again, Sophie. We've missed young voices around the place."

After we drop Marianne off at the nurses' residence, I tell Dr. O'Malley about my parents.

"You're a very brave girl," he says. He takes me to the front door and Aunt Em asks him in.

"Thank you for bringing me home," I say. "Night, Aunt Em."

Upstairs I divide the tissue paper from the box of chocolates into three squares. There are fourteen chocolates left. Four for Mandy, four for Nigel, four for Aunt Em, and two for me. I cut up the ribbon and tie up each of the little parcels. I put Aunt Em's on her bedside table, and Mandy's in my satchel to give to her in school tomorrow. I'll see Nigel after his cricket match.

Dr. O'Malley and Aunt Em talk for a long time before I hear her come upstairs.

· 20 ·

Uncle Gerald came down to London. He and Aunt Em and Dr. O'Malley consult endlessly about how to reunite me with my father. Uncle Gerald thumps the table and says, "Red tape. Stupid bureaucrats who do nothing but shuffle pieces of paper."

"Gerald, dear, you are not in a court of law. You don't have to convince us," Aunt Em says.

One afternoon three weeks later, Bridget, Marianne, and I are sitting in Bridget's garden. We've made lemonade from the first lemons to reach the shops in over a year. It would taste better with more sugar.

"Father's on a crusade. If he can help to bring Mr. Mandel over, he feels it would make up for . . ." She looks at Marianne. "You know, some of the people he couldn't help."

I keep telling myself how grateful and happy I am – I mean, I'd be a monster if I wasn't – but deep down I'm dreading telling Father I want to stay with Aunt Em.

Father and I write regularly to each other. More than anything else, it was the socks that pleased him.

The wool is so soft and new. I look at the beautiful gifts that you and Fräulein Margaret packed for me. I wonder sometimes if I am dreaming.

I have left the hospital now and am back in Berlin. The birds have not returned to the Grunewald. Trees are gone, cut down for firewood. Cities throughout Germany are flattened. Armies of woman – *Trümmer Frauen* – rubble women – work twelve hour days to clear the debris. I long for fields and trees and birdsong.

Father writes of people I've never heard of whom he's trying to locate. Each letter ends with the same words – that he's impatient to see me again.

I find it hard to know what to write about. It's usually a variation of the weather report and comments about his health. Aunt Em's not much help. She says I should write about my life, ordinary things. It feels dishonest somehow not to tell him about my plans to stay in England forever. I take Aunt Em's advice.

Mandy and I play tennis. Our Girl Guide troop is planning its
first overnight camp since the war. We're going to Windsor
Great Park. Nigel and I are helping to plan the Guy Fawkes
party. The first since 1939. November 5 is the anniversary of
the Great Gunpowder Plot of 1605. There'll be fireworks this
year and we'll be burning a huge guy – an effigy of the traitor
who tried to blow up the king and the House of Lords.

I write we're still short of food, queues for almost anything are
endless, and that large parts of London are bombed and laid
waste too. It's like writing to a stranger and the thought of
meeting him unnerves me. I can't talk about that to anyone, least
of all to Marianne, who is still mourning her father.

One Friday afternoon in late July, a few days before the end of
term, I find Aunt Em waiting for me outside school. She hasn't
done that in years.

"Is something wrong, Aunt Em?"

"On the contrary. Your father has been granted a temporary
visitor's permit. He'll be here in a few days. It's exciting news,
isn't it, Sophie?"

I wonder what Aunt Em really feels.

"Yes, it is." I do my best to sound enthusiastic.

Marianne and I manage to get a ten minute break together in
the cafeteria during my Saturday shift at the hospital.

"I'll be thinking of you next Saturday," Marianne says, when I
tell her the news.

"I'm frightened, Marianne."

"Don't be. I'm sure he's nervous about meeting you again too. Have you sent him a picture of yourself? Bother, times up. I've got to get back. We're horribly busy. Talk to you soon, Sophie."

I know I can't live up to being the only person Father's got left in the world. Being sorry for all he's been through is not enough to make me want to live in Germany again.

On Monday morning a letter arrives from the Home Office. They apologize for the delay, due to the many enquiries they receive of a similar nature, etc.

> In order to be considered for British citizenship, the present law requires a person to have lived in the United Kingdom for a minimum of five years and to have reached the age of twenty-one.
>
> However, we anticipate modifications to this law in 1946. The changes under consideration will permit young people who were forced to leave their homes and have lived in Britain for five years to apply for naturalization if they meet the following criteria:
>
> 1. They must be fifteen years or older and under the age of twenty-one.
>
> 2. Neither mother nor father are living.

They returned Matron's letter to me. *I'll just have to find enough courage to tell my father how I feel.*

· 2 I ·

He's arriving today! I didn't sleep at all last night. Neither Aunt Em nor I manage to eat lunch. Tea is ready to be wheeled in on the little trolley in the kitchen. "Perhaps he'd prefer coffee. I'll make some," Aunt Em says and leaves me alone in the sitting room, staring through the window, so I can open the front door the minute he arrives.

Dr. O'Malley's gone to the airport to fetch Father. It was decided he'd stay with the O'Malleys because his health is not up to managing stairs yet, and Dr. O'Malley thinks it'd be a good idea if he was nearby. Father will spend most of the day with us.

A car draws up outside. A frail-looking stooped man with white hair, wearing a suit that seems much too big for him, gets out of the car hesitantly. Dr. O'Malley offers his arm. I suddenly think of my grandfather.

"Aunt Em, they're here."

I rush upstairs, and fasten the Star of David necklace around my neck. Voices drift up the stairs. "No, thank you. I can't stay for tea, Margaret. I'll be back for you in an hour or two, Jacob, and then you can settle in."

I don't know how I get back down. In the hall we stare at each other, the old man and I. He moves toward me, and touches my hair.

"*Wie deine Mutter.* Like your mother."

Aunt Em disappears and we're alone in the sitting room. I've been practicing what to say.

"Papa. I've been waiting for you. Did you have a good journey? You must be tired. Please sit down." We sit beside each other. "I'm sorry, Papa, I've forgotten how to speak German."

"Don't be sorry. I am happy to speak English. Zoffie, you are a grown-up young lady. What a long time it has been."

"Yes. In English my name is pronounced Sophie. Sorry."

Now I have to apologize again. I shouldn't have corrected him.

He smiles at me, showing broken teeth. *Gaunt.* Now I know what *gaunt* looks like – it's this – those dark sad eyes watching me. I look away, afraid I'm going to cry.

I don't remember you at all. My real father is young and handsome and smells of pine trees.

I try not to stare at the bent fingers and thick knuckles.

Are you truly my father? Where is Aunt Em? Why isn't she here?

Father takes a grubby piece of paper from his pocket. It's been folded many times. He offers it to me. I'd prefer not to touch it. I do, of course. The paper is almost transparent. I look at the way his bony wrist protrudes below his shirtsleeve. He's wearing the white shirt I sent him from the Red Cross. I remember Mama ironing a clean shirt for him every day.

"Allow me, Sophie." Father unfolds the creases very carefully, as if afraid the precious paper might tear.

It's a drawing of a house. Two windows decorated with window boxes. Red dots for geraniums. A crayoned yellow sun shines in a bright blue sky. Smoke billows from the chimney in perfect circles. The house is surrounded by a neat fence. Stick figures walk along the path. A man and a little girl with a bow in her hair. The girl holds a red balloon.

The letters in the bottom right-hand corner are faded. I can just make them out: FÜR PAPA. SOPHIE 5.

He takes the drawing back, folds it again. Puts it away in his pocket.

"I kept it hidden – *immer* – always."

The days pass quickly. Papa and I gradually get to know each other again. There are so many things we can't talk about. When he looks at me, I can see him wondering where his "Zoffie" has gone, just as I puzzle about the half of my life he and Mama spent without me.

I show him my favorite places, though Papa can't walk very far yet. He loves the penguin pool in Regent's Park. "I knew him."

"Who, Papa?"

"Lubetkin – the man who designed the zoo. That was before he was famous." I'm suitably impressed.

Aunt Em drives us down to meet Uncle Gerald and Aunt Winifred. She gives me a long lecture about what she expects of me. I'm on my best behavior.

Papa is an instant success. He bows over Aunt Winifred's hand. For a horrible moment, I think he is going to kiss it.

"Let me show you my garden, Mr. Mandel." Aunt Winifred takes his arm!

Before we go home, Papa designs a rose arbor for Aunt Winifred, down by the place where the Anderson shelter used to be.

In the car on the way home, Aunt Em says, "How did you do that, Jacob?"

"Yes, Papa. I've never seen Aunt Winifred all fluttery like that."

Papa says, "She seems a charming lady."

I don't know my father well enough yet to know when he is serious or joking, so I keep quiet. Perhaps after the Nazis, everyone seems charming to him.

One afternoon we're in the garden. I'm weeding the border under the kitchen window, and Papa's resting, watching me from Aunt Em's old basket chair.

"How happy you must be here, Sophie," he says.

"I am, Papa." I sit on the grass beside him, scraping damp soil from my fingers.

"Have you always been happy with Miss Em?"

"Mm."

He's leading up to it. He's going to say it – tell me we'll be happy in Germany too.

"Mama and I hoped for this so much. Your happiness, until we could have you back home with us."

I jump to my feet.

I'm not brave enough to tell you, Papa. Not brave enough to say you left me too long. I can't go back with you! I love you, but I can't go back.

"My hands are filthy, Papa. I'll wash and then I'll bring down some of my sketches to show you, if you're not too tired."

"I have a better idea. Help your old papa up the stairs. I want so much to see your room, your studio."

Papa sits at my desk, catches his breath. "This is a beautiful room, Sophie. When I was a student in Heidelberg, I lived in a little attic room – up four flights of stairs. It was much smaller than this one. From my window I could see the walls of Heidelberg Castle. Germany was beautiful once. A good place to be an artist."

Papa looks at all my drawings carefully. Once or twice he makes a comment about perspective, or the shading on a face. "This one, Sophie, this one is my favorite. I like all your work, but this one is special."

"It's Parliament Hill on Hampstead Heath. I'll ask Nigel to frame it – he's really good at carpentry. I want you to have it, a present to remember me by."

The minute I say it, I know I shouldn't have. I didn't mean to blurt it out like that. It's as good as telling him I'm not leaving.

Papa looks at me. He smiles. *Does he understand?* We make our way downstairs, one step at a time.

I don't see how there can be a happy ending. Papa knows it too, that's why he hasn't said anything yet. We're all trying not to upset each other. No one seems to want to start talking about what comes next. Not Papa, not me, and certainly not Aunt Em. I'm under twenty-one. . . . I may not have a choice. According to the Home Office letter, I don't.

· 22 ·

This is Papa's last week with us. Aunt Em and I are having breakfast. Papa's coming at ten and we're going to the National Portrait Gallery.

Aunt Em cuts her toast into neat triangles. "When we started out together, Sophie, I tried never to think about this moment and how hard it was going to be to part with you."

"Please talk to Papa! Tell him you need me. Why can't he stay in England? Why has no one thought of that?. . . . Someone's at the door. Much too early for Papa."

"I suggest you go and see who it is, Sophie."

"Papa, you're early. Come in. We were just talking about you."

"Jacob, how nice. Would you like a cup of tea?"

Papa sits down. "Nothing, thank you. I have something important to tell you. It cannot wait. I cannot wait."

"Papa, I have something to say too. . . ."

I mustn't put off telling him any longer.

"You will let me finish, please, Zoffie?"

That old German name. I can't listen to this.

Aunt Em puts her hand over mine.

"Before I left Germany, when I was still in Munich, in the hospital, a nurse helped me to write a letter to the British Home Office. I told them about you, Zoffie – how it is important that we find each other, that we must be together because we are the only ones left, you and I."

Papa takes out a letter. "This arrived with the early post today. It is from the Home Office." He reads:

> We are pleased to inform you that the Ministry has agreed to extend your permit to remain in the United Kingdom indefinitely. After five years, you may apply for naturalization.

"Oh, Papa, it's wonderful." I throw my arms around his neck.

"Sophie, stop. You are choking me."

"I am very happy for you both," Aunt Em says, "for all of us."

"I am a lucky man. Do you know, Miss Em, your brother and Dr. O'Malley wrote on my behalf? They sponsored me. So now, I can begin again. A small studio, no stairs, I promise. I shall plan gardens, teach drawing. What do you think, Sophie?"

"Let's put up a sign: JACOB MANDEL – LANDSCAPE GARDENER."

"There is one more thing I want to say. Miss Em, dear Miss Em, Charlotte and I had Sophie with us for seven years, and then she came to you for another seven years. The question is, what shall we do with her now?"

This time I don't hesitate. "I think you should share me. I would like that very much," I say.

"I agree one hundred percent," Papa says. There is a pause.

"Thank you, Jacob." Aunt Em's eyes are bright. "That sounds like a perfect solution."

I live with Aunt Em and see Papa most days. He rents a little flat close to Hampstead Heath. We walk, and go sketching together. On Fridays I cook supper for him and I've learned to say the Hebrew prayer for lighting the Sabbath candles. Marianne joins us whenever she can.

It's hard for Papa to talk about the war, about the past.

"I want to ask you something, Papa. You don't need to answer me if you don't want to."

"What is the question?"

"How did you go on when . . . after Mama . . . in the camp, how do I say it?"

"*Aushalten* – Endure? Each day, in my head I drew a garden and I tell myself, one day I will find my Sophie. One day we will draw gardens together."

The End

Author's Note

Prewar Berlin and the war years from 1939–45 in England and Wales is the world I grew up in. It was a world of disappearances and good-byes that no one had time to explain to a small girl. Perhaps the adults did not have the answers.

I was the same age as Sophie when I left Germany on a *Kindertransport* for Britain. Like her, I carried a doll.

Finding Sophie is not my story. It is a work of fiction based on historical events.

Although most of the ten thousand children saved from Nazi oppression by the *Kindertransporte* were Jewish, they came from all kinds of religious and economic backgrounds.

After the war, many of the young people discovered they had lost one or both parents and decided to stay in the country that had sheltered them.